LTL

MURDER IN MACKINAC

✓

MURDER IN MACKINAC

A NOVEL

BY RONALD J. LEWIS

AGAWA PRESS
MACKINAW CITY, MICHIGAN

Additional copies of this book may be ordered through bookstores or by sending $12.95 plus $3.50 for postage and handling to:

Publishers Distribution Service
6893 Sullivan Road
Grawn, MI 49637
(800) 507-2665

Copyright © 1995 by Ronald J. Lewis
Cover illustration by Mary Blue
Cover design by Debra Anton
Text design by Heather Lee Shaw
Library of Congress Catalog Card Number: 94-72293
ISBN: 0-9642436-01

Printed in the United States of America

10 9 8 7 6 5 4 3 2

To my wife, Margie,
and to my sons, Jeff, Randy and Gary

Acknowledgments

My neighbor, Dr. Douglas Steere, was appointed by President Roosevelt to direct the assistance from American citizens and the U.S. government to the Finnish people, whose towns were ravaged by the Nazis on their retreat from Finland in 1945. Dr. Steere's stories about his assignment, told to me and my Finnish wife, became the inspiration for my plot.

To learn more about the actual accounts of Cmdr. Mitsuo Fuchida and Lt. Saburo Shindo, who led the attack of Pearl Harbor, read Gordon W. Prange's, *December 7, 1941, The Day the Japanese Attacked Pearl Harbor.* His meticulous accounts of the events of that fateful day, gathered from personal interviews and research, made it possible for me to accurately weave the *actual* details into *a fictional* mystery.

MURDER IN MACKINAC

1

THE white-haired old man shivered into con
sciousness. He was looking straight up at the
blinking red light on top of the tower pier, 300
feet above the roadbed of the Mackinac Bridge. He felt
pain in his lower back and under his neck as he twisted
his head downward to look into a Boris Karloff face. He
caught a glimpse of a muscular woman with menacing
eyes, urging the monster-like man to hurry. It took him
a moment to comprehend the shocking significance of
his position. His memory snapped back into place, just
as his 120 pound body was thrust out over the guardrail

of the world's longest suspension bridge, to plunge down 199 feet to the Straits of Mackinac.

It would take only three and one-half seconds for the body to reach the treacherous currents below and be separated from life on earth. In the first second, he worried about Dorothy; she would be lost without him. In the next second, he thought. "If I had only sent those papers to Harold? Now I'm the only one on earth who could have stopped them". And in his last one and one-half seconds, instead of moaning and groaning over his unfortunate situation, Toivo thanked God for his 82 good years, and appreciated what an exceptional view he had of the Mackinac Bridge.

•

It was Thursday, May 14, 1992. The leaves were bursting out on the trees as Roy Nelson was preparing for tomorrow's drive from his house in Mt. Pleasant, Michigan to Mackinaw Village on the Straits of Mackinac. After a cold, bleak winter the greening of the trees was a happy sight. Roy needed some cheering up. There were too many things around the house that reminded him of Eleanor, even though he had packed most of her personal belongings away months ago.

He reached in his briefcase for a key when his hand pulled out a tattered blue coupon with the date 1976 on the back. He turned it over and it read: *"Good for the enthusiastic delivery of one long hug and kiss any time you present this coupon."* Tears burst out and flooded Roy's eyes. He began to sob uncontrollably, gasping to catch his breath. His heart pounded in rapid irregular beats. He scrambled aimlessly around the rooms trying to control himself. Finally he calmed down, but continued to sniffle and sob for a good twenty minutes. Eleanor had given him that coupon, and he carried it in his briefcase for sixteen years.

Roy had managed to control himself after the tragic loss of Eleanor. He had tears in his eyes many times, but had not really let it out until now. Eleanor brought sunshine and happiness into his life. He enjoyed pampering her and waiting on her, and every success, every accomplishment was shared with her. He knew that his life could not be the same without her.

Yet, Roy's attitude toward everything in life had always been positive and happy. He wasn't quite sure why he couldn't cope with the loneliness after the crash at Detroit Metropolitan Airport, that happened only nine months ago. Because they were not able to locate her body or any of her belongings, and because there was a difference in the on board count and the official count, Roy held out that small ray of hope that she was not on the plane.

The Dean of the College of Business at Central Michigan University had awarded Roy, a tenured full professor of accounting, a research leave for the Winter semester. Roy had never taken a sabbatical, even though he had earned it. The research grant allowed him to take a break from the classroom and to complete his interviews of Japanese transplants in the auto supplier industry which he had started last Summer. Roy travelled throughout Ohio, Kentucky and Tennessee where the Japanese-owned suppliers were mushrooming around the Honda, Toyota and the Nissan plants. He returned to Mt. Pleasant in April to work on an article based on his research. He was anxious for warm weather so that he could head North to the cottage. And finally, he would be on his way tomorrow.

•

Roy looked at his watch. It was 8:55 p.m. At that exact minute the body of the frail, elderly man was falling, straight down, 199 feet into the Straits of Mackinac. Little did Roy suspect that his noncontroversial, nonpolitical, academic life would be plunged into turbulent chaos and life threatening entanglements, both controversial and political, from that moment on.

Earlier that Thursday, Toivo and Dorothy Makinen had just finished lunch in their sixty-five year old cottage in Mackinaw Village, at the tip of the Lower Peninsula of Michigan. Toivo was on the beach with a stale loaf of bread. Dorothy watched him as he broke off a piece and threw it up in the air. First one seagull was there swooping down, catching the piece of bread in his beak. Then there were two, three, and in five minutes a hundred gulls, swarming, screeching, dive bombing over Toivo's head. He loved it. He rapidly threw piece after piece, in the air. Dorothy gasped as he threw one straight over his head. As the bread was coming down, an enormous, grizzled old gull, with pointed beak wide open, at full throttle, grabbed it out of the air just three inches above Toivo's head. Dorothy chuckled to herself, "they never miss."

Dorothy looked even more petite in the main living room of their fieldstone cottage, standing in front of the huge stone fireplace reaching to the top of the vaulted ceiling, surrounded by knotty pine. The early cottages along the water to the West of Mackinaw Village were built as vacation homes in the late 1920s, 30s and 40s. The Makinens had already winterized their cottage with insulation and central heating because they liked to stay from May until November. They had also added a twenty foot long glass enclosed front porch, where they could relax and watch the thousand foot ore carriers and the ocean freighters pass by. Right now Dorothy was being entertained by two sailboats dancing on the waves over on the Upper Peninsula side of the Straits of Mackinac.

Toivo finished the loaf of bread, and waving both hands over his head, walked slowly away from the beach to escape the hungry gulls. As he was washing his hands he heard Dorothy answer the phone. "It's for you, dear."

"Hullo, Toivo, this is Henry, ya know, Henry Hakala. I'm here at the Grand Hotel, ya know, on Mackinac Island. Member, I wrote ya, said I'd call ya to tell ya what time ta come over. There's a few fella's here who want to see ya, and the Govner's gonna give us a little speech after dinner. Can ya come over, say in a coupla hours. It's real important, Toivo." Henry was a Finnish-born American. He spoke the Finglish common to the older Finns in the Upper Peninsula of Michigan.

"Dorothy, that was Henry Hakala, calling from the Island. I told him I would leave on the two-thirty boat. That way I'll get there at three and come back on the last boat. Henry said that the last boat leaves at eight o'clock. They added one special boat because of the conventions," Toivo explained to his wife of sixty years.

Although Toivo would never call it senility, Dorothy was showing signs of slowing down mentally, so he explained everything carefully to her. Dr. Makinen was eighty-two and Dorothy just turned eighty. He was a Professor Emeritus of Engineering at the University of Michigan. Their winter home was still in Ann Arbor, but they were much happier in their Summer cottage on the Straits of Mackinac. They had just arrived for the Summer season one week ago.

What Toivo didn't know was that Henry had informed Dorothy a month ago that he was to be the guest of honor and that the Finnish veterans would have the Governor present him with a plaque.

"Now don't worry, I'll be back before dark. It doesn't get dark until about eight-thirty or nine at this time of year. They really want to see me, some of the fellows were on the front lines with me."

"I know dear, you have to go. They'd be disappointed if you didn't."

Professor Makinen took the Captain Shepler, a ferry boat that left Mackinaw Village at 2:35 p.m. and arrived at the Mackinac Island dock at 2:55. The regal Grand Hotel carriage was waiting for him at Shepler's dock, thanks to Henry. The two perfectly matched Percherons lazily pulled the carriage up Market Street to Cadotte Avenue, past William Backhouse Astor's fur trading building of another century. Only on Mackinac Island could one live in the past, completely free from the rampaging automobile, while still existing in the present.

Professor Makinen would normally have noticed the deep, blue-green water of the Straits stretching to the Mackinac Bridge in the distance, the venerable Little Stone Church on the right side of the road, and at the top of the hill, a little to the left, the magnificent white front porch of the Grand Hotel. But, Toivo had seen this view many times and he had a lot on his mind tonight. The carriage pulled off to West Bluff Road that passes in front of the Grand Hotel.

Henry was there to meet the professor. "Hullo Toivo, is it Ok if we forget the ranks." Toivo had been Henry's commanding officer at the front.

"Of course, my good man, that was a long time ago. We're just friends now."

Henry and Toivo were World War II Finnish veterans, who had fought against the Russians in the war of 1939-40. Those who had later emigrated to Escanaba, Negaunee, Houghton-Hancock, Iron Mountain, Marquette and other small towns in the Upper Peninsula of Michigan, were having a reunion. There were only about fifty veterans left, but they had almost perfect attendance at their reunions. They were proud that their commanding officer had just been honored by the Finnish Government. So they had asked Governor Hansler to do the honors of awarding Toivo with a plaque from them, and to give a short speech at their reunion.

"Toivo, have ya met Govner Hansler?"

"No, I'm afraid I've been retired too long. The last Governor of Michigan I knew personally was G. Mennon Williams, Soapy, is what they called him. He was here for all the Mackinac Bridge ceremonies in 1957. I'm just not very active any more," replied Toivo. "It's a pleasure to meet you, Governor Hansler."

"It's my pleasure, sir. You must have been quite a hero to receive such a belated honor from the Government of Finland. The people of the State of Michigan are proud of you, and your friends here are a credit to your reputation. They must think a lot of you to ask me to bestow their special honor on you."

Toivo recognized the glib tongue of a politician, but thanked the Governor with sincere courtesy. Then he said, "Henry, you didn't say that I was to be honored, you old Soumilainen you!"

After the dinner and the short program Toivo and the Governor had time to walk around the enormous front lobby of the Grand Hotel. Professor Makinen quite unexpectedly said, "Governor Hansler, I have to talk to you in absolute private. Can you arrange for a private room, it's quite urgent."

"Of course, just a minute."

Governor Hansler walked down one flight of stairs to the registration desk and asked for the manager. He came back up a few minutes later with a key and joined Professor Makinen. There was a small conference room just down the main hallway. The two men entered the room. They came out fifteen minutes later, shook hands and parted. It was 6:30 p.m.

The Governor had completed his part of the program. He located Henry Hakala and excused himself.

"I'll walk back to the Governor's Mansion, Henry, it's not far from here. I'll have time to rest on the Island tonight, and then I have a busy schedule in Lansing, tomorrow."

"I'll bet ya always have a busy schedule, Govner, eh?"

The Governor was back at his Summer residence at exactly 6:50 p.m. Hilda, the brusque housekeeper was in the kitchen. She was anything but feminine, more like a Clydesdale workhorse.

"What would you like to eat?

"Nothing for me. They served us a gourmet buffet at the Grand, so I just gorged myself."

"Very well, and as long as you don't want anything, William and I will go over for a bite at the Keyhole Bar and Grill in Mackinaw Village."

The Governor knew that she and William, the groundskeeper, really wanted to sit and drink. He preferred to be alone anyway to prepare for a speech at Michigan State University in East Lansing tomorrow. He wanted to go to bed early in order to get up at 6:00 a.m. to make all his connections.

"By the way, I have to talk to you about something, Hilda."

Hilda recognized the serious look in the Governor's

MURDER IN MACKINAC   [9]

face. She followed him into the study and the Governor closed the door behind them. They were in the room for fifteen or twenty minutes. William could hear the angry, muffled, shouts by Hilda even from out in the front yard.

•

Professor Makinen waited in the lobby of the Grand Hotel. He was enjoying the music of a trio of violin, piano, and bass fiddle, playing old time favorites of the forties and fifties. At 7:25 p.m. he got up and walked through the front entrance. He hesitated momentarily, stunned by the enormity of the Oglebay Norton, a 1,000 foot self-unloading lake freighter, longer than three football fields, that was passing directly in front of the hotel. Toivo walked down the red carpeted stairs to the narrow street where the nineteenth century shiny maroon Grand Hotel carriage with its perfectly matched Percherons waited for hotel guests. He turned for a second to look back at the massive porch, and decided to walk the fifteen minute journey to the nearby Shepler dock.

He walked down West Bluff Road in front of the hotel and turned down Cadotte Avenue toward the water. A carriage, similar to the Island taxis, pulled by a team of Clydesdales stopped on the other side of the street and the driver, a large, muscular man, walked up to the professor and said, "this coach is reserved for you, Professor Makinen."

"Thank you, my good man, I am taking the special eight o'clock ferry, let's see... its at the Shepler's dock."

The carriage continued in the same direction, up Cadotte Avenue, instead of down toward the docks.

Before the elderly man objected, the driver said, "the Governor sent me to pick you up, sir; he wants to see you. He says it's important. It won't take long, he says, sir. And I'll take you back to Mackinaw Village in the Governor's launch. You won't be more than a half hour or so later, sir."

"Very well, but if its more than that, I'll have to call my wife."

The carriage turned right at Annex Road and proceeded to the Governor's Mansion. Officially it is called the Governor's Summer Residence, but most of the locals still call it the Governor's Mansion. The carriage stopped in front of the Mansion and the driver helped Professor Makinen get out. The woman called Hilda came out to help. They walked toward the back of the Mansion where there were tall bushes on both sides of the walkway. The driver grabbed the elderly man, putting one arm over his mouth to muffle him. Hilda injected him in the arm with a needle. They held him for a few minutes until he lost consciousness.

William and Hilda loaded the professor into the carriage and the Clydesdales started their slow journey down the winding road which led to the Mackinac Island Marina. Even though the Marina was not yet open for the season, which would begin on Memorial Day, there were open berths available for transient boaters. The Governor's private launch had its own permanent berth. The Governor had few opportunities to enjoy the launch, so he didn't object to William and Hilda keeping it in operating condition.

"Let's get him in the launch right now, while there's no one around to see us," Hilda said. They carried Dr. Makinen into the launch and prepared for the cast off. The horizon, visible beyond the two towers of the Mackinac Bridge, was on fire just before the sun was about to plunge off the edge of the earth. The indescribable red and orange reflections in the clouds slowly darkened to signal the beginning of the ominous journey. The Governor's private launch, a 39 foot wooden Chris Craft, left the Mackinac Island Marina at 8:15 p.m. It headed out of the harbor between the Round Island Lighthouse and the Round Island Passage Light, into the freighter channel. The cabin cruiser skimmed along the water aimed directly at the Mackinac Bridge for four miles and then turned to the South toward the tip of the Lower Peninsula. Thirty minutes later it docked at the uninhabited Mackinaw Village Marina.

William lifted the elderly professor out of the boat, while Hilda secured it to the dock. They helped to steady the older man as they half dragged him toward the Marina parking lot.

"It's good that shot lasted this long." William said.

"Did you get his keys?"

"Yes, and there's only a few cars in the parking lot. Let's try that old blue Chrysler."

Hilda took the keys and tried one in the door. It worked. "You're right, it looks like an old man's car; that was luck," William said, "there's my car, right over there." He pointed to a 1985 dark grey Audi.

The husky groundskeeper jammed the groggy old man into the front passenger seat of the Chrysler. He started the car and drove away from town to an entrance to I75 about two miles South of the bridge. At that point, where there was a five mile straight stretch of highway, William waited until no headlights were in sight. This would allow them the extra minutes they needed to accomplish their task. They would have to take their chances that there would be no traffic from the opposite direction. At this time of night and at this time of the year Southbound traffic was usually light.

He entered the thruway and Hilda followed in the Audi. It was dark when the two cars reached the middle of the Mackinac Bridge. William stopped the Chrysler and Hilda parked the Audi close in front to obscure its license plate. She hurried to the Chrysler.

"Any cars coming?" he asked.

"No, it's clear both ways; do it now, quick!"

William pulled Dr. Makinen, still groggy from the drug, out of the car. He picked him up and carried him to the edge of the bridge. He raised the frail octogenarian high over his head, poised to throw him far out, over the side. At this moment Toivo Makinen regained his senses.

The impact from the 199 foot fall would turn steel into putty; it meant instant death to the fragile human body. The currents at the center are so strong and the water so deep that a body will not rise to the surface for a long time, if at all.

In the Fall of 1991, a Yugo, with the body of a young woman in it, that had been the first car to ever go over the bridge, was brought up from the bottom by the Coast Guard. The impact of hitting the water at that height, falling from near the first tower, folded the car in half so that the two bumpers almost touched.

There was no traffic for several minutes. William and Hilda jumped into the Audi, made a U-turn over the median strip on the bridge, and headed back South to the Mackinaw Village exit. The blue Chrysler remained parked in the center with its motor running. The two perpetrators parked the Audi, unnoticed, at the Marina and took off for Mackinac Island in the Governor's launch. As they headed into the Straits toward the Island, they could see flashing red lights moving from St. Ignace to the center of the bridge. A Northbound truck driver had reported the incident at the toll booth, which is at the North end of the bridge. The patrol car had just reached the blue Chrysler, and the officer was looking in the car with a flashlight. A few moments later a Mackinaw Village police car, driven by Officer Paul Tamber, turned its flashers on and hurried toward the center of the bridge.

William and Hilda arrived at the Mackinac Island Marina at 9:35 and secured the boat in its permanent berth. Bessie and Al, the two Clydesdales, patiently nibbling on the grass at the edge of the park, were now anxious to return to their barn. This time they practically ran up the steep road in back of Fort Mackinac leading to the Governor's Mansion. William dropped Hilda off and drove them to the barn, a few hundred yards further up the hill. Hilda opened the front door with a key and entered. It was 9:55 p.m.

She shouted so the Governor would hear. "We're back; William is taking Bessie and Al to the barn. Would you like me to make you some coffee?"

The Governor of the State of Michigan, Raymond Hansler, answered, "No thanks, Hilda. You and William go ahead. I'm going to bed early. I have an important and very busy day in Lansing tomorrow. By the way, Hilda, I have to make that morning plane from Pellston. So we can't forget to tell William to get Bessie and Al by six o'clock in the morning in order to get me to the Island airstrip on time."

2

ON Friday, May 15, Roy would pack for his trip, avoiding as many of Eleanor's reminders as he could. Although it was impossible not to visualize her in her normal habitat around the house. He hoped that he could feel more relaxed at the cottage, but they had spent much time together there too. Roy knew that he would have to leave close to 5:00 p.m. in order to arrive at the Straits before dark. He spent all morning getting the house closed up and making arrangements for most of the summer. In the afternoon he ran around in circles talking to himself, "Eleanor, where would you have put the cooler? Should

I take blankets? How about pillows?" Eleanor had always done the packing. She was an expert. Roy had never paid attention. He managed to pull away from Mt. Pleasant at 5:15 for the three hour drive to the cottage.

Roy passed Indian River on schedule as he headed toward Mackinaw Village. This was the first time he would stay overnight at the cottage alone. He knew that it was going to be difficult, but he had to face the fact that his life had to go on. He knew that if he could conquer his loneliness at the cottage it would be over and he would be able to get his positive outlook on life back again. His thoughts repeatedly reenacted the tragedy.

He remembered that one stewardess stated that a woman had to deplane a few minutes before departure for something she had left in the waiting room by the boarding gate. The stewardess was called to serve a grouchy first class passenger and did not see the woman reboard the plane. But, the woman had plenty of time to get back. Nevertheless, the authorities listed her on the plane and assumed that she had died in the crash.

Roy thought to himself, "but why would she disappear? Could she have amnesia, like in James Hilton's classic novel, Random Harvest? At the end of the story Ronald Colman regained his memory and he and Greer Garson lived happily ever after. Isn't that the way Roy and Eleanor's story should end, too?"

She wouldn't just run away from him; they weren't having any marital problems. On the contrary, they were almost too happy. Roy always thought that perhaps their marriage was too good to be true; and now he felt bitter about the abrupt way in which she was taken from him. It left him sad and just a little depressed. He felt that he had no one to be proud and praise him for his accomplishments, when he published an article, or received an award. Roy remembered the semester he wrote notes of congratulations to professors he knew in the College of Business, and even one or two in other departments, who had recently published articles in the major journals. Their names had appeared in the University newsletter. Roy respected praise and recognition from his colleagues, so he assumed they would too.

He knew his three boys were proud of him and were especially thoughtful after losing their Mother. But, they were busy and didn't have a lot of time for ol' dad. The oldest, married son, was a lawyer in Atlanta, Georgia, the middle boy was going to graduate school, and the youngest was taking art classes, both at Michigan State University in East Lansing.

Besides, Roy was content with being alone. He and Eleanor had preferred to do almost everything together after the kids grew up. As he was writing, she typed his entire textbook manuscript during the past several years. They travelled together, and because Eleanor didn't drive, they always shopped together. Now he was glad that he never complained about it.

The last weeks of the Fall semester went by slowly and Roy was exhausted with the latest crop of students. The combination of the *me* generation, and the *moaners and groaners*, as Roy and his colleagues called them, was getting to bother Roy. Fortunately there were always some respectful, well mannered students in every class who made it all worth while.

Roy was tempted to witness to his religious and moral convictions, but he had a strict self-imposed policy of not preaching morality or politics in his classes, unless it was relevant to the subject. Occasionally he stretched his policy, like the time he was explaining the chapter on not-for-profit accounting. He suggested that campus promiscuity was just a form of not-for-profit prostitution.

•

"Thank goodness it's Friday," was on Martha's mind that afternoon. Martha Reed, head of the State Statistical Records Department in Lansing, had just pulled into the driveway of her $250,000 Georgian Colonial in Okemos, with two massive white pillars to announce its elegance. There was no man to greet her, even though she had four bedrooms, three virtually unused, a black Lincoln Towncar, an orange 12 year old cat, and overflowing bank and investment accounts. She looked at herself in the mirror. Her hair, still blonde, with a few grey streaks of course. But, not bad for a 48 year old woman.

She was more attractive now than when she was younger. Her figure hadn't suffered a bit. At five foot, seven inches tall, 130 pounds, she was a knockout in her navy blue suit, the color that gave its wearer the mark of authority. But Martha knew how to maintain her femininity. She wore a white frilly blouse to soften what she knew was a frightening, overconfident, autocratic personality. Just this morning she interviewed a male candidate for a professional position. The last quizzical comment he made was, "I would report to you!" She knew right then that he would not fit into her demanding managing techniques.

She opened the mail and dropped everything on the table in her haste to read the newsletter from Detroit's Mackenzie High, class of 1962. They announced that the thirty-year class reunion would be held at the

Walled Lake Country Club on Saturday, August 8. "There's Kay Evans, Joyce Shorr, Don Harp, Lloyd Cassidy, Eugenia, Virginia, and, and, Roy and ..... Oh, I just can't wait to see them all," her head buzzed. Then she turned the page of the newsletter and saw it. "Roy Nelson, Professor of Accounting at Central Michigan University, lost his wife, Eleanor, in the plane crash at Detroit Metropolitan Airport last year."

"Oh, how terrible, poor Roy. Eleanor was such a sweet person." Martha tried to keep her true feelings from evolving. Roy was probably one of the reasons she never fell in love, or married, or both. She had had a crush on the little boy next door since childhood. They once danced the Charleston together in a Noble School play back in the seventh grade. No one else was ever good enough for her. But she couldn't blame it all on Roy. Her erudite, opinionated, approach to the simple problems of everyday life scared most men away before she could ever develop any meaningful relationship.

"Would she now have a chance with Roy? It's a sin to even think about it after just reading about poor Eleanor's death." Sin or no sin, that prospect kept invading Martha's conscious mind. She wondered if she should call him or just wait for the reunion. She couldn't know that Roy's very life would depend on that intellectual mind of hers long before the reunion. And that she would soon be inextricably drawn into his life in a way that she would never have anticipated.

It was dusk when Roy rounded the curve after which the magnificent Mackinac Bridge would appear. Roy knew the exact spot on I75 when the bridge would come into view, mile 334, because he always offered five cents to the one in the car who first saw the bridge. His three boys waited for this moment each time the family drove to the UP to visit Grandma and Grandpa. But, Roy always seemed to see the bridge first so the poor boys never got that elusive nickel.

It was a clear night; the bridge was covered with red, white, blue, and amber colored lights. It was breathtaking. Man's most astonishing accomplishment; the longest suspension bridge in the world, from anchor pier 17 to anchor pier 22. Roy knew all about the bridge construction, even the numbers of the main piers. Although the distance between the two tower piers 19 and 20 was surpassed by the Golden Gate Bridge the true measure of a suspension bridge is the distance between the anchor points.

The bridge stretches across the Strait of Mackinac or Straits of Mackinac, as the locals and some scholars prefer it, a five mile wide stretch of water connecting Lake Michigan and Lake Huron. Ore carriers up to 1014 feet long travel the Straits to supply the hungry furnaces of the Gary, Hammond, Indiana steel industry, and bulk carriers from overseas up to a maximum of 750 feet long travel the St. Lawrence Seaway system to trade with Chicago, Milwaukee and other markets in the Midwest.

The sight of the bridge was enough to make Roy feel at home. He and Eleanor sat for hours just admiring the magnificent structure at night with the colored lights sparkling on the still waters of the Straits. Frequently in the Summertime after the sun goes down the water becomes perfectly still. It is then that the bridge lights are reflected on the top of the water in a rainbow of colors. This is a surprise to those tourists who have only seen the splashing waves and felt the cool brisk Canadian winds.

He looked forward to seeing Professor Toivo Makinen and his wife again. The retired professor and his wife were octogenarians and lived in the cottage next door during the season, which for them was from early May to the end of October. Professor Makinen had just been honored by the Finnish Government for his service in World War II, which had been delayed for some forty years. It appears that he was in the Finnish Secret Service during the 1939-40 War with Russia. He became entangled in a complicated situation when Finland sided with the Nazis to help keep the Russians from taking all their land. During the period that the Nazis occupied Finland, it became apparent to the Finns that they were as bad as the Russians.

In retaliation to the inhospitable Finns the German armies burned and ravaged the small towns in Northern Finland. The United States Government and private citizens were sympathetic with the Finns and supported them with private donations and whatever official help was allowed within our foreign policy. Since Finland was the only nation to pay its World War debt to the United States the American people had a special respect for the Finns.

Eleanor was a Finn from the Upper Peninsula of Michigan. She was a diamond in the rough. Her parents spoke English which was sprinkled with the usual mispronunciations resulting in a language fondly called Finglish by the UPanites. In spite of the great odds against it, Eleanor became quite sophisticated by reading avidly. Her Father was an alcoholic, so she and her Mother were the backbone of the family, which meant that instead of going to college Eleanor stayed home and worked to help support her family. Indeed, at that time, it was not expected in poor families that the girls would go to college anyway. By the time she met Roy, her sisters and brother were all grown up and on their own.

Dr. and Mrs. Makinen were fond of Eleanor, not only

because she too was Finnish, but because she was so thoughtful and likeable. Eleanor found something nice to say about everyone. No matter how humble a person's home, she would find one nice thing about it and compliment the person. Eleanor made a fuss over Mrs. Makinen's linens and her antique dishes.

Roy liked to hear the stories about WW II, but Dr. Makinen never mentioned that he was in the spy business. So it was quite a surprise when Roy heard that he was honored for his work in the Secret Service. The Professor had always implied that he was an officer in the Finnish army and he did not talk a lot about the overall war effort. Not unusual for veterans who witnessed the horrors of combat.

•

Roy turned off at the first exit in order to drive through Mackinaw Village, which after the tourists leave, has a population of only four or five hundred hardy permanent inhabitants. He drove along the waterfront and noticed the difference since he had last been here. There were new motels all along the main street; several restaurants had been remodeled and there were many new tourist-type gift shops. Although he was happy to see the expansion and especially the clean, modern look of the town, he was sad to see some of the quaint small town flavor disappear. The town was quiet in May because the tourist season didn't start until Memorial Day. The Grand Hotel on Mackinac Island opened in mid-May, May 13 this year, and would close during the last week in October.

It was a pleasure to see the empty streets; Eleanor had said that these were the times that the town was theirs, when they seemed to have it all to themselves. They had to live downstate in Mt. Pleasant because of Roy's job at Central Michigan University, but they both felt that the cottage was their real home. It was to be their retirement home, but now Roy wasn't sure if he would be able to enjoy it alone.

He drove around Fort Michilimackinac and was about to turn on Lakeside Drive toward the cottage when he remembered that he would need a few groceries and that he should pick up a local paper. He drove to the only grocery store in town to buy a few necessities.

"Well hello Professor Nelson," welcomed Claudia. We haven't seen you for a while. Are you going to stick around or just up for the weekend?"

"Oh, I think I'll stay a while."

Claudia was in her late twenties, rather an attractive girl, Roy thought. She was always friendly with him, and Roy knew one subject that never failed to interest young people, college. She had told Roy that she attended the junior college in Petoskey for one semester, but it just wasn't for her.

"You live on the beach down near the Makinen's, don't you?" Claudia remembered.

"Yes, they live in the cottage next to ours... mine," Roy wasn't sure if Claudia knew about Eleanor.

"Look at the headlines." She handed him today's, Friday, May 15, issue of the Mackinaw Journal. The headline was: "Dr. Toivo Makinen Missing: Feared Dead." The article read: "Dr. Toivo Makinen, famed Professor retired from the University of Michigan, is missing. Bridge authorities reported that a car registered to Dr. Makinen was found abandoned on the Mackinac Bridge at 8:45 p.m. on Thursday night, May 14. Mrs. Makinen told the Mackinaw Village police that her husband did not return from a meeting at the Grand Hotel on Mackinac Island earlier that evening. The incident is under investigation."

"Oh no," Roy's enthusiasm to have finally reached Mackinaw Village took a nosedive. His anticipation was shattered. He had so looked forward to chatting with Toivo and Mrs. Makinen. Even though they were recent, and still just casual friends, they were the only ones he could feel comfortable with in talking about Eleanor. Eleanor's relatives and close friends would become emotional and find that there was nothing to say to Roy. After all, Eleanor was the charmer. Roy always felt that their friends really liked her, even the men, and that he was just being tolerated. And he quickly found out that a single mate doesn't fit anywhere. So he had looked forward with anticipation to his visit with the old couple. What a letdown. But, cheer up old boy, he thought, you are used to shocks by now.

Roy paid Claudia for his groceries and the paper. "Do you know if the bakery is still open, Claudia?"

"It's Friday night, they should still be open until nine, you'll just make it in time; we do have a few hardy tourists in May, although its been cool this season, so far."

Roy drove down Central Avenue toward the water by Shepler's Ferry docks. The main street was newly decorated on both sides with Victorian street lamps and small trees with strings of tiny white lights, just like Disneyworld, he thought. He turned the corner and parked in front of the Mackinaw Bakery. The bakery was the town's meeting place. Many of the local contractors, city employees, and townspeople who worked in the shops, spent their morning break in friendly conversation, while enjoying their coffee and doughnuts.

Lillian spotted Roy coming in the door and reached for a loaf of salt rising bread.

"I know you want this. Anything else?" Lillian smiled. Roy always bought at least one loaf of salt rising, for toast, when he stopped at the bakery.

"Give me two raisin oatmeal cookies, and... a raspberry turnover... that should hold me over."

Lillian was the daughter of the folks who owned the bakery. She was in her early twenties. Her Scandinavian heritage was exposed by her unblemished skin and her straight blonde hair piled on top of her head. Roy knew she was bright and encouraged her to go to college, but like many of the local young people, she would rather stay and work in Mackinaw Village than become embroiled in the hectic life of the college towns, or work in one of the big cities downstate.

"Is this your first trip this Spring... I mean... alone that is, I know I haven't seen you, but we don't open til' halfway through April." Lillian had heard about Eleanor's death from Clayton LaCombe, Roy's other next door neighbor.

"Yes, I finally got up enough nerve to stay for a while. I have lots of writing to do. By the way, have you heard anything about Professor Makinen. The paper says that he is missing."

"Well, I just heard from the coffee gang that he is probably dead. That is, if he actually did go off the bridge. Nobody could live through that fall, they say."

Roy thanked Lillian and drove along Lakeside Drive to the cottage. It was only about a mile from town. There it was; a most beautiful sight for Roy's eyes. The quaint, wood sided, sixty year old, yellow cottage, with white trim and, in the Summer, red Geraniums in the window boxes, was right out of a storybook. And no cottage anywhere else had the magnificent view of the bridge from end to end, with the Grand Hotel in the background looking like a sparkling diamond.

Roy was home again. This was more like home than the house in Mt. Pleasant. After turning the water pump on, cleaning and straightening up a bit, Roy made some coffee. He ate his two cookies and one raspberry turnover while he watched the 11 o'clock news. Fortunately, he was so tired from the three-hour drive that he fell asleep without anxiety about returning to the cottage for the first time without Eleanor.

•

On Saturday morning Roy felt the weight of all that had happened. He was anxious to talk to Mrs. Makinen. He walked next door after his skimpy, but savory, breakfast of coffee and salt rising toast, and knocked on the door. Mrs. Makinen answered the door and couldn't suppress her happiness to see him.

"Oh Professor Nelson, I'm so relieved that you've come. I don't know what to do. I'm so worried." She hurried to get Roy a cup of coffee. She remembered how her husband and Roy always talked over a cup of coffee.

She was a petite woman, about five feet tall and very thin. Her concern over her missing husband was apparent, causing her to look even more frail and delicate than her eighty years would indicate. She and Roy had many pleasant chats in the past, so perhaps his presence would be of some comfort to her at this time. Mrs. Makinen proceeded to tell him the exact details of yesterday, when her husband failed to return home after his meeting on the Island.

"Toivo received a call just after lunch from Henry Hakala, who fought with him at the Mannerheim. He told my husband that the World War II Finnish veterans, who lived in the Upper Peninsula, were having a reunion at the Grand Hotel. Some of them had read about his long overdue decoration from the Finnish Government. They just wanted to talk about their war days. I think talking helps to get it out of their system. I know Toivo had nightmares for years after the war. Afterward, I learned that Henry and the other veterans wanted to surprise Toivo with their own award, a plaque of appreciation. So they invited the Governor to do the honors."

The Finnish Government had honored its war heroes shortly after the war, but Toivo was exempted temporarily to protect his identity. When he left Finland, the government lost track of him, so he never received recognition. Last year, one of his former students wrote a biography about the Professor and a copy was sent to Helsinki. Soon after the Finnish Government awarded him with a decoration of valor.

Mrs. Makinen continued. "Toivo was excited about the prospect of meeting some of his old friends. He said he couldn't have many personal friends during his secret service days, it was too dangerous. But earlier, he had spent several months at the Mannerheim Line, in the Karelian Isthmus, fighting the Russians after the November, 1939 attack. That's where he made some good friends."

She filled Roy's cup, and went on. "He left shortly after two o'clock. He said he would leave the car at the docks and take the 2:30 ferry over to the Island. Then he said that he would be home no later than eight-thirty or nine o'clock. He wasn't sure of the exact ferry schedule, and I can never find one of those daa...darn schedules when I want one. But, Toivo said that they added a special boat for the convention leaving at eight o'clock."

Roy noticed that it helped her to talk to someone. It must have been hard on her to sit in the house all alone, wondering what might have happened to her husband. "The paper said that Professor Makinen's car was found on the bridge." "Yes, Paul Tamber came over right away to tell me. Toivo had no reason to drive over the Mackinac Bridge, so why would his car be abandoned on the bridge? But Paul said they found no evidence of foul play, and the motor running...well, that occurs mainly in suicides, he said." Poor Mrs. Makinen was at a loss with the absence of a plausible explanation, other than suicide, and she just wouldn't accept that. Her husband, at eighty-two years old, was a threat to no one. The war was long past and he maintained no contacts with the Finnish Government to her knowledge. They had become U. S. citizens in 1955. His career as a professor at the University of Michigan did not involve any controversial or secretive subject matter.

"I just can't imagine why anyone would want to cause harm to Toivo," she said, tears filling her eyes.

While she and Roy were talking, her son and daughter-in-law arrived. Roy was relieved to have someone take over; he hated to leave her alone at such a strenuous time. He was anxious to talk to Paul Tamber, police officer and part-time security guard for the cottage owner's association. In Mackinaw Village it was necessary to have more than one job. Salaries for municipal jobs were low because of the small tax base. After Labor Day the village population dropped to a few hundred people. Paul was a good friend, and it seemed that everybody in town liked him. He had been hired by Roy to winterize the cottage and to open the water system in the Spring and close in the Fall. Paul's wife, Ruth, was a nurse who worked at the hospital in

Petoskey. Eleanor and Ruth liked each other and had quite a few tete-a-tetes over tea. Paul would know about the circumstances regarding Dr. Makinen's disappearance.

•

Paul was at the city hall building, which also housed the police station, the fire station, and the public bathrooms for the tourists.

"Professor Nelson, it's good to see you," Paul greeted Roy.

"You too, although I hear you had a rough night, Thursday. I just came from talking to Mrs. Makinen. Have you had lunch yet Paul? I want to talk to you about Dr. Makinen's disappearance; and I insist on treating you."

"No I haven't, but you don't have to do that."

"I insist. Let's go over to Kenville's. I haven't had a Whitefish sandwich for a long time. And by the way, start calling me Roy."

After Paul expressed his sympathy for the loss of Eleanor, Roy got to subject of the missing professor.

"I'd appreciate it if you tell me whatever you can, Paul."

Paul began, "well, it could be suicide, of course. But, I don't think so. Since 1957, when the bridge opened, there have been only two, or possibly three, suspected suicides. In 1974, the bridge patrol found an abandoned car near the middle of the bridge with the motor running. No body was ever found.

In 1985, a truck driver reported a car on the bridge with no driver in sight. I was on duty that night and drove out to the car with the bridge patrol. It was assumed to be a suicide.

And the third possible suicide occurred three years ago. A young mother disappeared after her abandoned car was found on the bridge. The husband said that she was despondent and contemplated suicide.

"Do you and the others, who investigated Professor Makinen's disappearance, think it was suicide or foul play?"

"We can't agree; the circumstances surrounding Makinen's disappearance do not point to suicide. He had no apparent reason to commit suicide, according to his wife. She said that he was in good health, for an eighty year old; they were perfectly happy; and they had no financial problems.

He had no apparent reason to be on the bridge. And I'm sure, at his age, he wasn't going around getting young girls pregnant, or some other embarrassing situation that old men kill themselves over. On the other hand, there was no sign of a struggle, and there's just no reason to believe that there was foul play at the scene."

"Were there any witnesses?"

"I talked to the truck driver who reported seeing an abandoned car on the bridge at about nine. He said that he saw the parked car and that no one was in sight, so he reported it at the toll booth.

"Did he say anything that might help?"

"Not really," Paul assured Roy.

"Anything else, what was the inside of the car like?" Roy asked, after a bite of his Whitefish sandwich. "Boy, this is good, did I miss the food in Mackinaw. Now I know why I like it here so much."

Paul thought a bit while Roy wandered off into his culinary distraction. "Umm, the only thing left in the professor's car was a piece of paper scribbled with the names of Henry Hakala, and the Governor, Raymond Hansler, and the numbers 2:30 and 1940. The paper was between the seats, and of course, could have fallen there at almost any time."

"Did Dr. Makinen see the Governor?"

"Well, the Governor was at the Governor's Mansion for the weekend and did make an appearance at the Grand Hotel to welcome the veterans. So, Makinen probably did see him."

Roy said, "let's try to talk to Henry Hakala and some of the veterans. Can you go to the Island with me? We can catch the 2:30 ferry."

3

Roy and Paul were on the 2:30 p.m. ferry to Mackinac Island. Paul had an annual pass on the ferry. Roy paid the round trip fare of $11.00. A young man collected the tickets on the boat as they headed across the Straits. Roy asked him, "were you working on Thursday?

"Yes, all day. It's slow in May, so I work on all the trips from Monday through Friday, but not on week-ends."

"Do you remember an older man, in his eighties, going over on the 2:30 and coming back on the special eight o'clock boat, last Thursday?"

"I know what you're getting at. It's that guy who jumped off the bridge, ain't it? Paul here, he already asked me some questions."

Roy apologized, "Oh, I'm sorry Paul. I should have asked you."

"No, no that's OK. I figured you might as well hear it from him. By the way, this is Professor Nelson, Jake; he teaches accounting at Central Michigan University."

"Oh my God, don't talk about accounting. They made me take it at the junior college; it was terrible. Anyway, it's nice to meet you."

"Same here, now you started to say something about Thursday," Roy continued.

"Oh yeah, well May is when either the high schools or the senior citizens take tours. It's off season, just like in the Fall. So there was a tour on the 2:30 boat. They were all older folks and I couldn't tell by Paul's description if that guy was on the boat or not. I hate to say it, but with their white hair and mustaches, and their polyester clothes, those old guys all look alike to me. As for the eight o'clock, I just didn't notice anyone in particular. Paul said, "thanks Jake. See Roy, we know that he took the 2:30 ferry over, and we have to assume that he took the eight o'clock back."

It was Saturday, May 16, and the Finnish war veterans would still be at the Grand Hotel. The Island fascinated Roy. It was the single most enjoyable tourist attraction for him, no automobiles. It was wonderful to walk or ride a bike on a road and know that a monstrous hunk of metal with a half crazed, self-appointed race car driver at the wheel wasn't going to run you down. Roy remembered the day that he and Eleanor were riding bikes on the Island and passed a young boy who had fallen off his bike and was badly bruised. His mother and dad were helping him. A few minutes later a man, dressed in a police uniform looking like a London bobby, came rushing to the scene of the accident furiously pumping his bicycle. It wasn't supposed to be funny, but they couldn't help laughing over a sight they would see no where else in America.

And on their last visit to the Island they witnessed a runaway horse team. Where else could you see two huge Belgian draft horses pulling a wagon with two frightened drivers at the reins racing out of control down main street filled with tourists who, hearing the thunderous clop-clop of the massive hoofs and the shouts of the frantic drivers, scramble out of the way just in time. The only other way to witness this scene is to find a time capsule that can take you back to the nineteenth century. Mackinac Island is truly unique.

The two friends walked to the great hotel, known for its long porch and its beautiful surroundings. Roy and Eleanor had loved its respect for the past; the absence of telephones and television sets in the rooms; and they especially enjoyed the four o'clock high tea. The pair entered the hotel, Paul using his police credentials to avoid the five dollar fee that the hotel now charged to tourists. They were able to locate the organizer of the Finnish veterans reunion, Henry Hakala, and arranged to meet him for lunch at the golf course dining room.

Henry Hakala was in his late sixties; his face reflected the "SISU", a Finn word to explain the determination that allowed a small Finnish army to turn back a massive Russian force in the winter war of 1939-40. He had been with Dr. Makinen at the front.

Henry Hakala told them, "Toivo was one smart commanding officer, eh! We was outnumbered, ten ta one...maybe twenny, but he tricked dem Rooskies inta goin on... what ya call... a wild goose chase, one after da udder. But we knew we was gonna hafta fall back every time we attacked em. There musta been millions of em. So we built saunas on the way up and stopped to enjoy em on the way back."

In early 1940 Makinen was transferred out of the front lines. Henry never saw him again until Thursday afternoon. Henry helped Roy and Paul to locate and talk with other veterans who knew the professor at the front, but nothing more was learned that would shed any light on why the professor disappeared. One of the veterans, named John Kivela, had heard Dr. Makinen and the Governor talking about the honor bestowed on the professor. Kivela had seen the two of them going onto a private meeting room, but, he didn't have any idea how long they were there. Roy and Paul returned to Mackinaw Village on the ferry, knowing that they had not accomplished much. They had certainly not learned anything to help explain why Professor Makinen disappeared.

•

On Sunday Roy visited Mrs. Makinen and asked, "Do you think it would help if I go through your husband's papers in the small cabin in the woods."

Dr. Makinen had the cabin built in the woods a few hundred yards behind the cottage for his writing. He apparently required complete privacy and quiet while writing his several books and numerous articles over the years. Roy hoped there would be some clue that might explain the good professor's absence.

Mrs. Makinen said, "You probably didn't know, Roy, but Toivo never allowed anyone in his cabin alone, including me. I've never used the extra key he kept in his drawer until now."

She handed it to Roy and blessed him for his concern and help. As Roy started to insert the key, the door opened with only a slight push. Someone had already been in the cabin. Perhaps their son had been inside to look over his father's work and for personal memorabilia. But, one quick glance confirmed that it was no friend who searched the cabin. An examination of the door revealed that it was easily forced open; the wood had deteriorated with age. Papers were strewn over the floor and there had been no effort to straighten up after an obvious search of all the drawers and shelves which housed the Professor's work.

Roy was now convinced that it could be no coincidence that first the Professor would disappear, and then his private cabin would be broken into. He spent the next few hours looking through the papers. They consisted mainly of the Professor's notes and reference material used in his research. Roy also found the envelope from a recent letter from Harold Martin in Honolulu, but the letter itself was missing.

The good Professor had introduced Roy to Harold Martin three years earlier. Roy had received an appointment to teach a master's level accounting course at Kaneohe Marine Corps Air Station on the Windward side of Oahu. The course was taught every other weekend over a five week period. The Professor suggested that Roy contact Harold and his wife, Dora, in case they wanted to visit the mainland during the same time period. As it turned out the Martins were delighted to have housesitters in order to visit Dora's family in Michigan.

Harold Martin was now eighty-four. When he was in his sixties he lost his first wife and later married Dora, who was slightly younger. Dora had never married until she met Harold, who was indeed a delightful man. Harold had made his fortune in the construction business and purchased a spacious lot on the ocean in the early sixties. His property was now valued in millions, not thousands anymore, thanks to the inflow of Japanese purchasing power in the eighties.

Roy and Eleanor were housesitters for the Martins in the Summers of 1989, 1990 and again in 1991. It was quiet and peaceful at the house and Roy was able to complete several chapters of his textbook while in Hawaii. It was understood that they would have no overnight guests, which helped Roy and Eleanor to refuse the many relatives and friends who would just love to spend a week or so in Hawaii.

Roy told Mrs. Makinen, "I'm sorry to tell you that the cabin was broken into and your husband's papers were strewn all over the floor. Do you have any idea what they might have been looking for?"

"I can't imagine, there's nothing of value that I know of."

Her son and daughter-in-law had no idea why, other than vandalism. The furniture was old and Dr. Makinen would never allow a television or even a radio to disturb his work. They offered to straighten up the mess, for their mother.

"By the way," how did Dr. Makinen and Harold Martin become acquainted?"

Mrs. Makinen replied, "Harold was with a division of the Corps of Army Engineers which was sent to help the Finns after the Nazis pulled out. Toivo and Harold spent almost two years together helping to rebuild the Finnish towns. My goodness, they were friends for more than forty years."

Since Roy knew that they had both taught at the University of Michigan he had always assumed they met there. Although Harold Martin did not have a doctorate it was not uncommon in those days for even The University of Michigan to hire experts to teach selected courses. And Professor Martin was a nationally known civil engineer.

Roy had already been approved to teach at Kaneohe Marine Corps Air Station for five weeks beginning on May 22. He taught there once before in 1989. He would surely want to talk to Harold about his experiences with Dr. Makinen in Finland during and after World War II.

Mrs. Makinen returned to Ann Arbor where she had a memorial service for her husband, presumed dead. She obligingly had the service on a day that Roy could attend since at their age the Makinens had very few friends and close relatives left, and she admired Roy for his attention to and concern for the old Professor. She gave Roy the key to the small cottage so that he could further examine the contents for clues to the disappearance of her husband. She still had a glimmer of hope, just as Roy did for Eleanor, that her husband was still alive.

4

FINALLY it was Tuesday, May 19, time to go to Hawaii. Harold and Dora Martin were leaving for California and Michigan the day after Roy arrived to housesit. Roy planned on spending the evening of his arrival talking with Harold about Dr. Makinen. Roy flew from Lansing on United Express in a small propjet, and from O'Hare, on a nonstop, straight to Honolulu. He had always remarked to Eleanor that there could be no nonstop flights. All flights had to have at least one stop.

The flight to Honolulu was almost nine hours. It was

tiring for everyone, but when the tourists, who had never been to Hawaii, caught that first glimpse of the islands, they burst out clapping. This was Roy's fourth time so, although he shared the elation of being in the beautiful Hawaiian Islands again, he considered himself a Kamaaina, not a tourist, so he tried not to appear as excited as the others. He buried his head in his briefcase instead of peering out the window to see the crater of Diamondhead, which the pilot was pointing out to the passengers.

The Islanders have a complex system of classifying everyone. There are some pureblood Hawaiians, who number a few thousand. They can trace their ancestry back to King Kamehameha I, or some other royal family member. There are numerous Hawaiians who are a mixture of polynesian, and some combination of Chinese, Japanese, Philippine, or other asian peoples. They consider themselves the locals. The permanent, or long-term residents, of European stock are called Kamaainas as differentiated from the tourists. Roy was not really a Kamaaina because he stayed only five or six weeks to teach his graduate class, nor was he a tourist, so he called himself an honorary Kamaaina.

As the plane was landing Roy spotted the large pink buildings of Tripler Army Hospital, where he taught in 1988. The main hospital building was impressive, high on the lush hillside above Pearl Harbor. It served its purpose, although not completed until shortly after World War II, as a military hospital for the wounded of the Korean and the Vietnam wars. It continued to serve as a military hospital for the Pacific basin.

"Oh my goodness, is that the airport?" asked the skinny young bride seated next to Roy.

"No, that's Barber's Point; it's a naval air station that serves to watch for submarines. During the *cold war* there were routine Russian submarine missions around the islands to monitor the movements of the U.S. fleet. Of course, everything is changing now with the end of the USSR."

Roy stopped himself. It was hard for him to give a short answer. He would usually give a lecture on the type of planes that Barber's Point had, and the fact that the base was bombed during Pearl Harbor. But, Eleanor would have tactfully interrupted to save the poor questioner from one of Roy's fifty-minute lectures. Fortunately he remembered her humorous interruptions so that neither his feelings would be hurt nor would the innocent questioner suffer the lecture. The young bride was more than satisfied with his explanation and now turned her attention back to the landing.

"Oh, we're going to land on the water!"

"Don't worry," Roy assured her. "When the wheels touch there will be ground under them."

There was the thump of one wheel and then the other and the tourists cheered and clapped. After nine hours in the air they were just as happy to put their feet on the ground as they were to finally be in the paradise they had been reading and hearing about most of their lives.

As before, Roy rented a car at the airport and headed out toward Kahala to the home of the Martin's. He drove along Nimitz Boulevard because he couldn't stand to go on the thruway the first day. After a day or so he could accept the inevitability of the thruways, but for his first view of Hawaii he had to drive through downtown Honolulu, along Ala Moana Boulevard to Waikiki, around Diamond Head, into Kahala, where each house along the waterfront is valued in the millions rather than in the hundreds of thousands.

The Martins had a mere 80 feet of ocean front property in Kahala, between Diamond Head and Koko

Head. Kahala contains Oahu's most valuable property. In 1990, one of the Martin's neighbors, just a little closer to Diamondhead, sold a 4000 square foot lot, with 80 feet of ocean frontage, for $4.4 million. That's $55,000 per foot. Roy's waterfront property on the Straits was selling for $200 per foot.

Roy drove into the Martin's circle driveway. Harold and Dora were happy to see Roy, even though they were saddened by the absence of Eleanor. After exchanging the formalities and enjoying the fresh fruit lunch which Dora so fussily prepared, Roy was anxious to delve into Harold's recall of over forty years ago.

"How was your trip? Dora asked."

"It sure was tedious. I would rather stop at the coast like you two always do, but I just take whatever flights they give me to get the lowest fare."

Harold and Dora didn't have to worry about low fares, and Harold at his age couldn't take the long flights. They routinely stopped off at San Francisco, where Dora had a neice, before going on to Michigan. The two men relaxed in the comfortable study while Dora diplomatically busied herself elsewhere in the spacious house. It wasn't really a house as people from the mainland think of. It was more of a system of walls and jalousie windows designed to direct the trade winds through the rooms to cool the inhabitants. Harold was proud to explain to first time visitors how the wind moved through the house as the designer had planned. Its beauty was in its spacious rooms and the openness.

The view was breathtaking, the ocean, Maunalua Bay, Koko Head and Koko Crater were visible from all of the main rooms. The other rooms opened onto lanai's with potted orchids and other flowering bushes and trees. Harold had been cross-breeding orchids since his early thirties and had several hundred potted orchid plants in the garden area.

"Harold, when I called you about Dr. Makinen's disappearance last Thursday, I didn't give you all of the details. I wanted to discuss it with you in person so we might figure out why he disappeared so mysteriously. I think it has something to do with his past."

"You mean at the University?"

"No, I have a feeling that there is some connection with his duty in the Finnish secret service back in World War II. First, he had a phone call to go to a meeting of Finnish war veterans, and then his car was found on the Mackinac Bridge. But, he had no reason to go across the bridge at that time of night. Dorothy was waiting at home in Mackinaw late at night. So he wouldn't go gallivanting around St. Ignace on the other side of the Straits at his age. Would you?"

Roy was a little embarrassed at his own last question, since Harold was also an octogenarian. Harold let it slip by and said:

"I don't know of any specific reason there would be a connection. But there may be one possibility; the two of us were involved in one extremely secret mission. Toivo was in charge of the mission for the Finnish secret service, and he was not allowed to tell me any details. I was ordered directly by General Eisenhower's headquarters in Britain to arrange for the transportation of a woman in her late twenties or early thirties, with two children, a boy and a girl, out of Finland. I arranged for their transportation to Austria and then to Switzerland, with the cooperation, but not official approval, of the U.S. government. I just assumed that they were political refugees, probably Jewish, and that we were helping them to escape the Nazis."

"There is one more thing," Harold continued. "Toivo told me years later at the University of Michigan that he secretly kept one of the communications which accompanied the transfer. He said that everyone who knew about the secret mission, except the two of us, was probably dead."

"When is the last time you talked to him about the war years?"

"Why he called about one year ago, I can't remember exactly which month it was, but, he did say that he wanted to send me a copy of the communications regarding that mission."

"Did he act as if it were something of importance today, over forty years later?"

Harold said, "well, he acted mysterious and definitely wanted me to have a copy of those communications, as if someday they might be important. So they could be of some significance, if we assume that Toivo's disappearance was foul play rather than a freak accident."

"Did he send them to you?" was Roy's inquisitive reaction.

"No, he must have forgotten, which indicates that they were probably not very important in the first place, don't you think?"

"Maybe so, since we aren't at all sure that there isn't some other reason, like robbery or ... whatever." Roy did not even convince himself of the 'whatever' possibility. He really couldn't think of a plausible explanation.

"When I was looking through the cabin I found an envelope from a letter you recently sent to Dr. Makinen," Roy continued. "Do you remember what you wrote to him?"

Harold pursed up, and rubbed his chin for a bit and then recalled, "most of it was just the usual chit-chat, but I do remember mentioning the war and how fortunate it was that we met and became friends. I was in a nostalgic mood and recalled some of the more humorous episodes of our wartime days together."

"Do you remember if you mentioned the woman and the two children in your letter?"

"Why yes, when I come to think of it, I did say something like, it seems strange that Toivo and I were the only ones left who knew about that secret mission with the woman and children. Oh, and I asked if he forgot to send me those communications."

Roy, not wanting to alarm Harold, did not mention that the letter was missing from the envelope. After all, Dr. Makinen may have failed to return the letter to the envelope. But Roy had that uneasy feeling that the prowler who broke into the cabin took that letter from the envelope and just threw the envelope on the floor where Roy found it. And that possibility made Roy very uncomfortable. Could there be a connection? He would not pursue it any further because he might unnecessarily alarm Harold. "Well, you'll need some rest for your trip tomorrow, Harold. Let's get some sleep."

The two men were both tired, Roy from jet lag and Harold from the normal aging process. So off to bed they went, Dora outlasted them all, watching the ten o'clock news by herself.

Roy drove the pair to the airport on Wednesday morning and waved goodby as the plane took off for San Francisco. A Hawaiian three-piece band was playing for the tourists who were pouring out of the gates. The tourists looked disheveled after their long flight, but they were happy to have finally arrived. Whenever Roy spotted the couples, young or old, with their matching Aloha shirts he couldn't resist saying under his breath, "darn tourists".

And how sloppy the new generation, dressing like bums no matter where they went. He realized that times were changing and he was becoming less and less able to cope with it. He just could not accept the widespread corruption in business and government. He could never understand how any rational human being would take 'rat poison', as he called any form of dope, willingly. He would never understand how any decent human being could throw trash on our cherished ground, especially beautiful Hawaii. And he could not take the maniacs who climbed up his back or passed him going 20 miles over the speed limit as he drove defensively along trying to obey the law. Oh, for the good old days, he mused, knowing that our parents probably had these same feelings, perhaps for different reasons.

The hula dancers snapped him out of his nostalgic trance. They were swaying with the traditional music of the islands. This is one place where the old traditions are cherished by the Hawaiian people. He remembered the wonderful lunch with Eleanor at the Willows Restaurant two years back. It was an unexpected treat. Thursday at the Willows is entertainment day. Irmgard Ilulu and her family usually provided the Hawaiian music, but this Thursday the Tutus had their end-of-the-year party.

The Tutu-ladies, defined as 'Hawaiian grandmothers and elderly aunties that have the last word and make the final judgments and pronouncements,' had voluntarily spent time in the schools teaching the children the songs, dances, customs and traditions of their culture. At the end of this particular school year they reserved several tables at the restaurant. One after another the Tutus were persuaded to get on the stage and entertain. Roy and Eleanor were thrilled as they witnessed the genuine spirit of Hawaii that most tourists would never see. The authenticity of the movements, the songs, the mumus and hats of these pureblood Hawaiians was spellbinding. After the lunch and entertainment one of the Tutu-ladies gave Eleanor her own handmade lei making her day one never to be forgotten.

5

ROY'S assignment was to teach his management accounting course to the military students, mainly flying officers, at Kaneohe Marine Corps Air Station on the windward side of Oahu. The course met on Friday evening and all day Saturday for three weekends, two weeks apart. The class started on May 22 and ended on June 20. He commuted from the house, which was on the leeward side, along the ocean past Hanauma Bay and Waimanalo Beach to the Marine base at the tip of Mokapu point, and sometimes returned over the Pali Highway or the Likiliki Highway through the mountains, for a change of view.

After one of his Saturday classes at the Kaneohe Marine Base one of Roy's students, a Colonel, asked him if he would like to see the Boobies. Roy blushed, not knowing that Boobies were birds, and awkwardly formulated an ambiguous, noncommittal answer. After being assured that the Boobies had feathers and wings, he agreed to go.

The Colonel, who was the Commander-in-Charge of the Marine Base Target Practice Range, made the arrangements for him to go to the Marine base on a weekday after the target practice stopped in late afternoon. The Red-footed Booby Colony is situated on top of the target practice range. The inside wall of dormant Ulupau Crater, about 700 feet high, shields the inhabitants of the base from any stray shells, and the oceanside wall, which rises about 400 feet above the sea is the home of one of only three known Red-footed Booby Colonies. Roy received a special VIP pass for entering the Marine Base that day, which to his amusement said, *Purpose: Visit Booby Colony.*

Mokapu Point juts out between Kaneohe Bay and Waimanalo Beach, and with the Koolau mountains in the background is one of the most beautiful sights in the world. Roy drove along the shore of the huge base to the firing range and walked up to the buildings. There were 'Restricted Area' signs all over, but his special pass gave him confidence to proceed. He was met by Sergeant Johnson who explained that he would be Roy's escort on the tour in the absence of the Colonel, who was called to duty elsewhere. The Sergeant and Roy boarded a Marine Jeep and drove to a flat area about half way up the crater wall where the road ended. Sergeant

Johnson parked the military vehicle and they walked in front of a large tunnel in the side of the crater wall. Sergeant Johnson explained that the tunnel was excavated shortly after the Japanese attack on Pearl Harbor.

At the time of the infamous attack, Kaneohe was a Naval Air Station with 33 PBY's and 36 Catalinas. Only three Catalinas were on patrol on Sunday morning, December 7, 1941. There were 334 sailors and 96 Marines stationed there. The airfield was bombed at 7:48 a.m., seven minutes before Pearl Harbor was hit. Sixty of the planes on the ground were destroyed and six damaged by the two waves of Japanese bombers and strafers. The Japanese lost two planes. It was a logical place for the invasion, which appeared to be imminent in the minds of the military leaders on the Island.

The cavern was large enough to hold two-hundred or more soldiers. Sergeant Johnson led Roy through the tunnel with a flashlight. There was no electricity and little had been changed since 1942. Outside the tunnel again Roy saw young Boobies on the limbs of the trees. They would not move from their perches, even if you walked within two or three feet of them. If a baby Booby falls from its perch the parent Boobies will abandon it.

All of a sudden the two men heard a disturbance in the tall brush. Roy glimpsed what turned out to be a Mongoose scurrying through the grass. Their presence had disturbed two young Boobies who fell off their perches. The Sergeant lunged out and grabbed one of the Boobies, which could not yet fly, and with a free hand called for help on his portable radio. Within a few minutes two Marines arrived in a vehicle and chased around in the brush.

Boobies were all around; there were about three hundred Boobies in the colony. As they walked up the path they passed within a few feet of the perches. The baby Boobies are covered with soft white, down-like, balls of fur. After two months, their feathers become an ugly smoke gray; and three years later their feathers turn white again for life. The adult Boobies have colorful red feet, the mark of the Red-footed Booby, and their beaks are a soft blue color with a pink border.

At the top was another surprise, Penn Battery. The massive big gun turret of the battleship Arizona had been taken from the sunken ship shortly after the attack and placed into the crater wall. It was placed into the ground three stories deep. Sergeant Johnson warned Roy about the area at the top of Ulupau Crater where there was no guard rail around the edge of the cliffs or around the open turret. The entire area is off-limits to everyone, unless escorted by a Marine guard.

The whereabouts of the big guns that were taken from the Arizona's turret is unknown. They were probably placed on one of the battleships, repaired and returned to action, but there is no record of what had actually happened. There was a great deal of confusion after the attack and keeping records was, quite understandably, not one of the top priorities.

At the end of the ridge was a cement machine-gun enclosure. A ladder inside the enclosure descended three stories to the barracks below. This was the extent of the defense effort, one machine-gun nest and one big-gun turret. Fortunately for the defenders there was no attempt by the Japanese to invade the Hawaiian Islands.

At the top Roy noticed the view. Toward Honolulu you could see Rabbit Island, beautiful Waimanalo beach, and Kailua beach. Northward was Kaneohe Bay and Chinaman's Hat, a breathtaking view. Now he knew why these rare birds had selected a small arms firing range for their home. They had one of the most spectacular views in the world.

On the way down to the tunnel level Sergeant Johnson explained, "did you notice that big plastic bubble in the tunnel, Professor? Well it's filled with water, several thousand gallons. About three months ago one of the shells from the firing range ricocheted back to the Booby side of the crater. It accidently started a brush fire that spread quickly over the Booby Colony. The Boobies remained in their perches, by instinct, and about sixty were killed by the fire. We were all so upset that we had to do something. Someone thought of the bubble idea. We just had to save those Boobies in case of another fire."

6

ON Sunday evening, June 21, a well dressed oriental man walked around to the back of a Mitsubishi automobile dealer in San Francisco. He adroitly dismantled the alarm system and enabled the locked door to yield to his illicit skills. He quickly located several sets of marked keys and exited to the outside lots. It took him only a few minutes to match a set of keys with a used 1991 dark blue Mitsubishi four door sedan. He drove the borrowed car to a shopping center and parked next to a public phone.

Harold Martin received a phone call in his room in the Fairmont Hotel at 9:00 on Sunday night. The caller's voice had no perceptible accent. "This is a friend of Professor Toivo Makinen. It was his last wish, before he died, to give you an important written communication. He wouldn't tell me what it is, but he asked me to give it only to you, and asked me to tell no one else about it. I promised Toivo that I would get it to you somehow. Meet me at the Tadisch Grill just down the street in ten minutes and I will give you Toivo's papers."

Harold decided not to worry his wife about the call. "Dora, that was a business friend who wants some personal advice. He wants to meet me at the Tadisch Grill; I'll be right back in half an hour. Don't worry."

Harold walked down the street toward the restaurant. The well dressed oriental man was parked on a narrow side street in the dark blue Mitsubishi automobile. The motor was running and he had a white scarf wrapped around his head. He slowly drove out of the side street. When Harold crossed the street to go to the restaurant, the driver sped down the street and smashed into him, sending him flying into the pavement.

The driver had selected a relatively secluded location where there were no witnesses. He pulled the scarf from his head as he drove off and disappeared into the traffic a few blocks away. A couple leaving the Tadisch Grill from down the street saw a car disappear around a corner, but could not identify it. Harold was taken to the hospital and died during the night.

Roy's class ended on Saturday, June 20. He had spent Sunday lounging in the sun, under the palm trees, by the ocean at the Martin's house. His grades were all calculated and he had nothing more to do for the course. Harold and Dora would be arriving on Tuesday afternoon from San Francisco. He slept soundly on that Sunday night. The phone woke him up at eight-thirty on Monday morning, June 22.

"Professor Nelson, this is Dora's niece, Jennie. I have some bad news. Uncle Harold was hit by a car late last night; he died early this morning, they said 3:30." Aunt Dora wanted me to call and say that she'd call you later to let you know when she'd be coming home."

Roy quickly calculated that it would now be about eleven-thirty, a.m. in San Francisco. Roy asked Jennie, "How did it happen? Do you have any more details of the accident?"

Jennie replied, "Aunt Dora said that it was a hit-and-run driver. She said that Uncle Harold received a phone call at about 9:00 Sunday night, to meet a businessman, at least that's what he said, at some restaurant nearby. He was only a few blocks from the hotel room when he was hit."

"How's your Aunt? Is she alright? It must have been a terrible shock."

"She was given some pills by the doctor. It... it was horrible. She has been crying a lot ever since it happened. She just calmed down in the last hour or so."

"Well, tell her to call when she's up to it. I will stay at the house as long as she needs me. Goodby, and thank you for calling."

"Goodby, Professor Nelson."

Roy noticed that she said Professor, not Mr. Nelson. Harold and Dora made it a point to let everyone know that their housesitter was a professor. They were from the old school, appearances meant a lot to them. Having a professor for a housesitter gave them a type of satisfaction that would not be understood by a new generation that has lost respect for both age and intellectual achievement.

Roy was a little frightened as well as shocked by the events. It was no coincidence. Dr. Makinen disappearing and now Harold killed by a hit-and run driver. Roy was uncomfortably aware of the implications. His reliance on probabilities in his own classroom demonstrations prompted him to accept the conclusion that both men were deliberately selected for their fate.

But why? He knew that he had no involvement in whatever linked the two men. Yet, he might be the only person who could recognize the connection between the two murders, assumed or otherwise. The perpetrators of this foul play might assume that Roy knows whatever it is that caused the two friends to be expendable. But, there was nothing he could do about it; for now, he had to housesit until Dora called. He would have to wait until he returned to Mackinaw Village before investigating further.

That evening Roy knew that he would go to the Royal Princess Hotel after dinner. Luana would be dancing at the Pink Orchid Room, which was an open lounge and dining area facing the ocean. Luana Kameha was a former Miss Honolulu whose mother was a casual friend of Roy and Eleanor. During their visits to Oahu they had befriended Tamar Kameha, who told them where to go to see the real Hawaii, not just the tourist traps. Tamar had suggested that they might enjoy listening to authentic Hawaiian music and hula dancing at very little expense.

Tamar had told Roy and Eleanor, "The Royal Princess is the fourth oldest hotel in Hawaii. It was remodeled in the early 80's and is now one of the most beautiful hotels in Oahu. The Pink Orchid Room is right by the water, and as you watch the show, Diamondhead is in the background. There is no cover charge; and you can just order a sandwich and a drink, or iced tea, and sip it all evening. And by the way, the girl dancing the hula is my daughter."

Roy and Eleanor went there several times and got to know Luana, who was as sweet as her mother. Luana was in her late thirties now, but her exotic Hawaiian beauty, a mixture of Polynesian, oriental, and caucasian was striking. Roy arrived at the hotel at about seven. He felt comfortable and nostalgic there because Eleanor liked it so much.

He had never really known where Tamar lived, or her phone number. Eleanor took care of those things. Roy knew that Luana would give him the information on her mother, and he wanted to tell them both about Eleanor. When Luana finished her dancing she always walked to the back of the open restaurant to her dressing room. Roy stood up as she approached his table. He was surprised that she immediately remembered his name.

"Aloha, Professor Nelson, so nice to see you again, but where is your lovely wife?"

"I'm sorry Luana, but I just didn't think about letting you and your mother know about Eleanor. She was killed... well, she was reportedly killed in a plane crash, not quite a year ago, in Detroit. But, they never found any evidence of her... her body, that is, or her belongings, and there was a difference in the count of the people on board and the official list of passengers. So I just don't believe that she's gone, yet. I won't believe it until I have definite proof."

"Oh, I'm sorry, Luana, here you are, practically a stranger, and I'm raving on about my problems and feeling sorry for myself."

"No, no, that's alright; Mother and I liked your wife so much. She was one of the sweetest and most thoughtful persons; we used to talk about how wonderful she was. I'm truly sorry, and please don't consider me a stranger. By the way, everyone calls me Luana. I'd like it if you would too."

Roy fumbled an apology, "I didn't mean it that way; I didn't realize, before now, how much you and Tamar liked Eleanor."

Luana contemplated for a moment, "I'm going to hate to tell my mother about your wife; you don't mind telling her, yourself, do you?"

"No, and it's my place to tell her, not yours. I hope I get to see her soon."

Luana wasn't just humoring this poor fellow; she honestly felt terrible about Eleanor, whom she liked so much; the two women had some memorable talks together. Eleanor was so motherly to Luana, and she always found something nice to say about her dancing, or her dress, or just her smile. Luana now realized that she had hardly noticed Roy; he was like background music for Eleanor.

Luana was used to aggressive, abrasive, and usually offensive male attention. Roy was definitely an exception; after he met Eleanor, he was never tempted by any other woman, no matter how beautiful. His professorial ethics were so strong that he looked upon his female students, many of them attractive and seductive, as little girls. He had a natural and effortless resistance, which protected him from temptation.

Roy knew what protected him, though it might be difficult for some to understand. He felt strongly that he had a God directed responsibility to his wife. When he had children, his responsibility to them was paramount. No personal, selfish desire was as strong as these responsibilities, and to be unfaithful to his wife was tantamount to abandoning his children.

When the children were in their early teens Eleanor suffered long periods of severe depression. It was difficult for Roy, but his commitment to his children helped him through the tough times. After a while, Eleanor was her old self again, and Roy was so glad that he hadn't given up. Since that time they were closer than ever, and appreciated each other even more. Roy believed that God expected him, as a husband and father, to hold his family together regardless of the adversity. He was convinced from his own experiences that adversity, which might destroy people with little or no strong religious faith, only strengthened people with a strong faith. It was necessary for the development of strong character and commitment to moral principles. The acceptance of sexual immorality by modern society was merely a sign of weakness and selfishness.

Roy was born in 1943, he would be 49 in October. He was not handsome, although the women who admired him said he looked like Paul Newman. His Swedish-Welsh heritage may have contributed to his appearance of self-assurance and dignity. He was in good physical shape, about 5' 10", and he dressed neatly, even in Hawaii.

Luana saw him as a man for the first time. She had admired him for what he represented, but now she was impressed with his physical appearance. She was a little embarrassed because she wouldn't think of showing her feelings. They were stronger than she wanted them to be. After all, this was a man whose wife was almost like a mother to her.

After some discouraging experiences with men, Luana never married. The men who pursued her were too obviously attracted only by her physical beauty. She inherited, from her mother, an extraordinary intuition about men, that allowed her to sense the insincerity of the numerous aggressive suitors she had in her younger days. Unfortunately, the type of man she wanted was often too shy to pursue her.

She noticed the way Roy treated Eleanor and had once said to her, "the reason I haven't married, Mrs. Nelson, is that I haven't been able to find a man like your husband." Eleanor had replied, "Don't say that so Roy can hear you; he'll get a big head." Subconsciously, Luana realized that now he was free. But, of course, Roy had told her that Eleanor could still be alive. Luana couldn't resist the thought that, "he's just wishful thinking." Then she realized how foolish a person's thoughts are, they sometimes take you for a wild goose chase into all kinds of weird places before you know it. Here she is with a casual friend whose wife has just died, and she has these strange thoughts about him. How stupid!

Roy had a compelling need to tell someone about the strange series of events. He was finding out rather abruptly that sharing feelings and secrets, that no one else knew, was one of the intangible assets of marriage. He wanted to share his secrets with Luana.

"Luana, I need to talk to you about something. Would you have time?"

"Of course, I have almost an hour before the last show. We can stay right here and talk, but, let's get a table down by the water."

It was 8:30 and the restaurant had thinned out considerably, so they found a nice private table with the ubiquitous million dollar view of Diamondhead.

Not having the faintest idea what Roy wanted to talk about, Luana took a chance on a little humor to break the seriousness of the situation. "Are you going to ask me out to dinner?"

"No! That is, well, of course, I would like to... but that's not what I... " Roy finally laughed, "I have been a little serious, haven't I? Let's take that up later."

"Luana, I'm involved in a very serious situation. I'll just give you a brief picture now. When I arrived in Mackinaw Village back in May, I found out that my next door neighbor had died mysteriously. He was supposed to have jumped off the Mackinac Bridge. But, the more I looked into the facts, it appears that he was probably murdered. He was in his eighties, and had been involved in some spy operations in Finland, back in World War II."

Luana's attempt at humor was ephemoral. She focused her attention on Roy's seriousness.

Roy continued. "By the way, did you know the Martin's, the people who own the Kahala house we stay in?"

"Not really, only what you and your sweet wife told Mother and me; that they were elderly and went to visit relatives while you were housesitting."

"Well, anyway, my neighbor, Dr. Makinen, is the one who knew the Martins, and that's how we got the housesitting job. It turns out that they met in Finland, working together on some joint mission during the war.

This morning, I received a call from a neice of Harold's saying that he was killed by a hit-and-run driver in San Francisco. Oh, and one thing I forgot to tell you. When I was looking in Dr. Makinen's things back in Mackinaw Village, I found an empty envelope from a letter that Harold Martin had written to Professor Makinen. The letter was missing and the cabin had been broken into."

"You mean that there was some connecting link between the two men, maybe even back to World War II, and now they are both dead? It can't just be a coincidence. If I can help in any way, just let me know. I have some time off coming and I'll be glad to work with you. It sounds like a mystery and I love a mystery. Please let me help!"

"Luana, I don't want to place you in any danger. It's quite possible that my connection with these two men could be misinterpreted by whoever killed them, even though I know virtually nothing."

It just dawned on Roy what he was doing; he wanted her to get involved. Was he already lonesome for female companionship? Was he attracted to that beautiful face? And, he hesitated to even consider it, was he attracted to the rest of what came with the face?

No! Luana was just a convenient friend, and he felt comfortable with her because they could talk about Eleanor.

Luana looked at her watch, "I want to help, and I'm not worried about danger. Oh darn, I have to get ready for the last show; meet me Wednesday for lunch at the China Garden, at noon. Goodby for now."

Before Roy left the Royal Princess and returned to the house he watched Luana dance the hula. The Hawaiian hula is the slow version, where the hand and arm movements are the main communicators of the dancer's story. Roy felt a twinge of guilt as he watched the sensual movements of the curvaceous enclosure that God had provided for this former Miss Honolulu.

He had never hesitated to tell everyone that if Eleanor died before him, he would never remarry, nor even be attracted to another woman. Of course, he never expected Eleanor to die so young. He fully expected that he would go first, or that they would both live well into their retirement age. Nevertheless, he remembered his strong statements, and had no doubt that he would keep this commitment. No doubt at all.

Luana had to dance out of pure instinct because she couldn't stop thinking about what she had said. What audacity!

"Meet me!" she said. Not, "perhaps we could get

together sometime to discuss this matter, Professor Nelson."

Or not, "perhaps you would like to come to the show and visit with me again, sometime?"

She didn't even say, "would you like to meet me?"

No, she said, "meet me!" And she even told him where and when. What nerve! But... he didn't say no, did he?

7

THE next morning, on Tuesday, Roy decided to have breakfast at King's Bakery. Tamar had told him and Eleanor that King's dining room was patronized by the resident Hawaiian people rather than the tourists. Roy had never been there alone so he called Tamar and invited her and her husband to join him. Tamar met him, but her husband was, as usual, on a freighter somewhere in the Pacific Ocean.

Luana's father, Walter Kameha, was a mixture of European and Hawaiian stock. He was born in Waimanalo on Oahu and was a teenager working for a shipping company in December, 1941. Like many residents he was sleeping in on the Sunday morning during the infamous bombing of Pearl Harbor. Walter was now a First Officer for Olson Shipping Company which transported most of the foodstuff and other materials into the islands.

Roy had an academic interest in transportation costs and he enjoyed watching the movement of barges into Honolulu harbor. He was amazed at the way a small tug pulled one barge filled with *fishyback* containers at the end of a long hawser, and at the end of a another hawser, a second barge. The barges appeared to be about 1,000 feet long. He couldn't understand how they made it across the ocean; they appeared so top heavy.

It was fun to eat at the King's Bakery restaurant; the people were fascinating for a mainlander to watch. Roy loved the pancakes and the sweet bread, which he guessed originated from the Portuguese. He ordered the pancake sandwich, an egg on top of a stack of delicious pancakes, the likes of which could not be found on the mainland. Tamar ordered Eleanor's favorite, the 'local boy', which had a hamburger patty covered with gravy and an egg; Roy didn't like it at all. Tamar adored Eleanor and was openly distressed by her death; she asked for as much information as Roy could give.

There was no question that Tamar was the mother of Luana. She was probably in her late fifties; she was the epitome of Hawaiian dignity. It was like being in the presence of an exotic Polynesian queen. Tamar was as trim as her daughter. And she looked no older than 39, but that is what Roy always thought about Eleanor too. He was amazed that he noticed so much about these women now; he never did before. She qualified as a pure Hawaiian; even though one of her ancesters had been of

Norwegian stock.

"Tell me how Luana became Miss Honolulu, Tamar. I've never even thought to ask her about it."

"When Luana was sixteen she won the Miss Teen contest at Waimanalo. The next year she won the Miss Kailua contest and didn't even place in the top ten in the Miss Hawaii contest. She really matured during the next year, at eighteen, and she won the Miss Honolulu contest. She was second runner up in the Miss Hawaii pageant, and that was the end of her beauty contest days."

"What was she like as a little girl?"

Tamar lit up, "oh, she was a sweet little thing. She loved the water, swam every day. She was as good, or better, than the boys, at swimming and surfing. And she was smart in school. She liked biology, especially. All about the island plants and the fish. That's what she liked best. And she wanted to learn all the Hawaiian customs and dances from the Tutu-ladies. She loved it when they came to the school, all the kids couldn't wait for the Tutus to come."

"Well, thank you Tamar. I'm going to meet Luana for lunch tomorrow at the China Garden, why don't you come too."

"I'd love to, Roy, but I still work part-time at the store. Remember the Kitchen Gourmet in Hawaii Kai; your wife loved it."

Tamar worked at a retail kitchen store in Hawaii Kai, next to the grocery store where Roy and Eleanor shopped. She worked to keep busy because her husband was gone for such long periods. In fact, that is how they met Tamar. On their first trip to Hawaii she waited on Eleanor, who seldom bought anything, but loved to browse, and the two women became friends.

"Remember the time we had lunch at Dolly Parton's

restaurant in Hawaii Kai," Tamar recalled.

"Yes, it was called the Dockside Plantation; I ordered those huge shrimp dipped in egg batter. And you two ordered the scallops. I still can't understand why her place didn't make it. The location was right, it had her backing and the food was delicious at a reasonable price. Yet, with all these positive marketing factors she ended up selling it. I sure loved those shrimp."

The restaurant business was a mystery to Roy. As an accounting professor he wanted an orderly solution to every problem. And any business problem should follow a pattern so that the outcome can be predicted. Not so with the restaurant business. One restaurant out in the boondocks can be a smash, while one in the best location possible can fail. One with excellent food and reasonable prices can flop, while one with overrated food and skyhigh prices is profitable. Dolly's restaurant wasn't in Waikiki, but it had a good location. Another restaurant in the area had a waiting list most of the time.

"Well that's marketing," he mused to himself, "I'm glad I stuck to teaching good old cut and dried accounting."

King's Bakery was a popular restaurant with the locals. It didn't depend on the fickle tastes of the tourists. Roy and Tamar finished their breakfast; Tamar gave Roy the customary kiss on the each cheek and they parted.

Roy drove downtown and decided to go over the Pali Highway to the Windward side of Oahu. Pali Highway cuts over and through the Koolau Mountains from Honolulu to Kailua and Kaneohe. At the top is the Nuuanu Pali Lookout, a tourist attraction overlooking the Windward towns and bays and Mt. Olomano. Roy pulled off at the tourist drive that ascended to the

Lookout.

The Pali Lookout is situated at the edge of a cliff, the site of the 1795 battle in which King Kamehameha I vanquished his opponents and conquered Oahu in his quest to unite the Hawaiian Islands. His soldiers literally pushed the defending army over the cliff to the rocks below.

On their first visit to the Pali Lookout Eleanor wore a skirt, she never wore slacks because Roy liked her to look feminine. She spent the whole time trying to hold her skirt from flying up, and was never able to reach the edge of the cliff. Even for Roy the wind was too strong to stand up straight. He had to crouch over in order to walk to the edge.

Roy drove into the parking area. There were a few buses and cars in the lot. Tourists were walking around the park, some leaning forward as they walked toward the edge of the cliff. The tourist area consisted of a stepped, walled platform made of poured concrete. The wind was not quite as strong as it had been on his earlier visit. Roy walked to the edge to relish the magnificent view. He could see as far as Mokapu Point at the end of the Kaneohe Marine Air Corps Station, and off to the left he could see Chinaman's Hat.

There was a stairway to a lower level, which was not visible from the top. He descended the stairs to see what the view was like from below. There were no tourists in sight. The walkway led to a vantage point with a panoramic view. There was only a waist-high metal railing between him and a long drop below. He was not fond of heights. A mist from the ocean was moving in fast and was beginning to slightly obscure the view.

As he stood looking, his body flipped over the railing and he hurtled downward. Somehow he was stopped by a ledge about twelve feet below. He was able to pull himself securely on the ledge to keep from sliding further down. A few more feet and he would have dropped hundreds of feet to his death. While he lay there, motionless, he could still feel the two hands on his back pushing him up and over the rail. Hearing muffled voices above, he remained absolutely still for ten or fifteen minutes. He was sore, but he knew that no bones were broken. He managed to stand up, though his ankle was twisted a bit.

Roy climbed up the side of the cliff and grasped the lower part of the railing. He was able to climb back onto the walkway. He ascended the stairs cautiously and eyed the tourists for any suspicious actions, even though he didn't know what to look for. It appears that no one was even aware of what happened below.

And as Roy well knew, because of the powerful wind, most tourists make it to the edge, take a quick look, and then retreat back to their vehicles. Roy managed to hobble back to his car and drive back to the house. He then took a shower and fell asleep for the rest of the day and all night.

•

The phone woke him up the next morning. It was Dora.

"Roy, my niece Jennie told me that she called you about the terrible accident. Harold's body will be cremated here in San Francisco and will be buried later in Honolulu. We will have a memorial service for the family members here. I won't be back there for several weeks. I am going to stay with my sister for a while. This has been quite a shock."

"I hope you know how badly I feel about Harold. He was one of my favorite people."

"I do know, and he enjoyed your company, too, Roy. Please call Bill Tsui, who worked for Harold, and he and his wife will take care of the house. Then you can leave whenever you wish. I know you must be anxious to return home."

Roy was not as anxious as Dora might think. He must find out what happened at the Pali. He noticed that it was time to get ready to meet Luana already, but he was still sore from the fall. Luana was right there at the China Garden at noon. They walked in and Robert seated them. Robert Chan was a legend, and his restaurant was a favorite of the locals. Numerous celebrities ate at Robert's authentic Chinese restaurant.

Robert was always nice to Roy and Eleanor. They were in Honolulu only for five weeks each year, and went to the China Garden two or three times each trip. Nevertheless, Robert remembered them and had the waitress give them free dessert, always the Almond Beancurd with mixed fruit.

Last year he made headlines in Honolulu when a man entered the restaurant, pointed a shotgun at him and demanded cash. Robert grabbed the barrel and wrested it away from the robber, who fled down the street. He was captured a few hours later. His waitresses said that Robert was perfectly calm and unaffected by the frightening incident. Robert's bravery was the talk of the town for a few days.

Robert also had the reputation of knowing everyone in Honolulu, including the shady characters. Roy began wondering if he might be helpful in unraveling the mystery of his near demise. First, however, he must tell Luana what happened.

"Luana, after your mother and I had breakfast at King's, I decided to see the Pali Lookout. I love that view. I was on the lower level, you know how it is, there's a narrow walk with a metal railing around the outside. Well, someone tried to kill me. They actually pushed me over the railing, but I luckily fell onto a ledge that broke my fall and saved my life."

Roy took a sip of Oolong tea the waitress had automatically delivered to the table, as if to allow Luana to absorb the significance.

"It had just started to mist up, so whoever did it must have thought they succeeded in killing me. Otherwise, they could easily have waited for me to climb up and just push me over again. I had a hard time holding on as it was."

Upon hearing the details, which were fairly brief, Luana intuitively put her hand on Roy's hand; a delightful tingle went right through him.

She said, "Oh, Professor Nelson that was terrible, you were almost killed. Now you know there's a connection between the two deaths, and that they both must have been murder. And we (she switched from you to we, Roy noticed) can assume that they, whoever they are, are convinced that you have some threatening information."

She had a motherly, or was it a daughterly, look of tender concern in her sparkling brown eyes, which, surrounded by her exotic mouth and long, black, silky hair, caused Roy to be very uncomfortable. His innate resistance was letting him down. He reached in his back pocket in order to release his hand from her touch without appearing too obvious. He pulled out his handkerchief to give his movement an apparent purpose. Luana pretended that she was completely unaware of her effect on him.

"Robert, can you sit with us for a few minutes," Roy called. Robert asked one of the waitresses to man the cash register while he sat down with them. Roy gave him a quick picture of the situation, and in detail what happened at the Pali.

"I know a little about your influence here in Honolulu, Robert. Is there any way you can help me... us, to find out who tried to kill me?

Robert spoke his English clearly, but with Chinese intonations. "Our system is capable of tracing anything unusual going on in the underworld. Honolulu is unique from all other American cities. Movement on and off Oahu is easily traced because it is an island, and also because most of the open land belongs to the military bases. The Chinese, Korean, Japanese and Philippine Hawaiians are loyal, patriotic Americans. We have cooperated in establishing the Information Network Center, generated to monitor the movement of international criminals into Hawaii, particularly into Honolulu. Our main concern, of course, is drug traffic, but the system is capable of exposing all forms of, shall we say, undesirable activities."

Robert explained further that he is the coordinator of the network. Information is funnelled to him and he distributes it wherever necessary. The informal group never does anything illegal, and merely transmits the information to the police when the situation calls for action. The group has an unofficial approval from the prosecutor's office.

"I will have information on any new movements by tomorrow," Robert offered. "I better get back," he added, and returned to his register.

Roy and Luana ordered the Singing Rice soup, which came in a large bowl, big enough for two people. The waitress poured the hot broth filled with pork and oriental vegetables over the hot rice; the steam shot upward with a loud sizzle as heads turned to watch. That made Roy's day.

[72]   RONALD J. LEWIS

Roy never knew how to order from Robert's authentic Chinese menu, so he let Luana do it. She ordered some kind of crepes that you fill with what appears to be Chinese vegetables and pork, and add a sweet and sour sauce made with molasses and soy sauce; then you roll it up and eat it like a taco. It had been Eleanor's favorite dish at the China Garden, "Ill bet she told Luana," he thought. When they finished, the waitress brought each a dish of Almond Beancurd, and said, "compliments of Robert."

Roy paid the bill and said, "thank you for the dessert, Robert, here's my phone number at the Kahala house."

Luana said, "I'm dancing tonight; come arou...that is, would you like to come and nurse a sandwich and a pot of coffee, and then I could visit with you during my breaks."

"OK, Luana, I'd love to. Did you hear that, Robert, I'll be at the Royal Princess tonight, in case you call."

Luana was excited, "I'll call my Mother to come too. Dad will be gone for at least another week and she gets lonesome. Do you mind picking her up if she wants to come?"

"No, of course not, and why don't you have the trio join us, too."

The trio consisted of three of the Island's senior musicians, who played only the more traditional Hawaiian music for Luana's dancing. She sprinkled in a few of the fast Tahitian hulas once in a while, but the entertainment was meant to be slow and relaxing, not loud and frenetic.

Roy enjoyed talking with the three elder Hawaiians about the good old days, and especially about what they saw when Pearl Harbor was being bombed and afterward.

Roy picked up Tamar and they drove to the Royal

Princess. During one of their breaks Luana and the elderly trio sat with them. Sam Akaka looked like a septuagenarian and the other two men were probably a few years younger. Roy noticed that the oriental Hawaiians frequently used Hawaiian names for their girls, but seldom for their boys. They chatted about the trends in music and, of course, how they hated to see the Japanese buying all the oceanfront hotels except the Hawaiian Hilton.

Sam said, "I'm at least half Japanese, so I'm not prejudiced against the Japanese nationals, but the prices of our property and our food are rising steadily. Us Hawaiians and even the Kamaainas won't be able to live here much longer."

The others agreed but had no solutions. Luana was signaled by one of the hostesses. She left and returned quickly saying, "it was a message for you, Professor Nelson, from Robert, he said to meet him at noon tomorrow at Wo Fat's."

8

ON Thursday, June 25, at noon, Roy drove to Chinatown, his favorite part of Honolulu. The city had done a wonderful job of cleaning up the area, without destroying the cultural beauty. Wo Fat's Restaurant was the center of the intrigue. Several years ago, on his first teaching assignment to Hawaii, Roy and Eleanor had lunch at Wo Fat's, only to learn that there is no Wo Fat. He does not exist. Hawaii Five-O made him up. What a shock.

Another shock, Wo Fat's was the meeting place for Robert's sub rosa Information Network Center members. Robert introduced Roy to George Tong, owner of the Pagoda Hotel and Restaurant. There was absolutely no one in sight in the enormous Wo Fat dining room, which was on the second floor. Roy had not even noticed that the restaurant was closed for lunch that day, until he saw the empty room.

George led them through the kitchen to a back stairway, which went back down to the first floor. At the bottom of the stairs were two rugged looking oriental men playing cards. There was a large steel door at the other side of the room, which George opened with a key after one of the guards inserted his key. Roy observed that it was just like his safe deposit box. The room on the other side of the door was filled with electronic machines.

George explained, "Professor, this is the most sophisticated information network in the world. We have cooperation from every country in the Pacific Rim, except Cambodia and Viet Nam. Although we haven't had full cooperation from Japan in the past, a high level Japanese official recently asked for our help. He heard about our capabilities and requested that we cooperate, with whom he called the law abiding Japanese officials, in a very secretive joint sting operation. It seems that the honest government officials and businessmen are planning an all out attack on the underworld in Japan.

We also have cooperation from England, France, Italy, the Netherlands and all of the Scandinavian countries. Germany, Israel, Ireland and most of the moslem countries won't cooperate. The old USSR would never join our system, but now we are approaching the newly formed nations. The local and state police and the FBI cooperate informally by feeding us information as long as we don't get into enforcement."

George continued, "We analyze the movements of all

illicit arrivals and departures into the Islands. Our computer system will isolate any abnormal patterns of the American, European, Chinese and Japanese mafia. These are the major groups. We also monitor numerous minor groups of drug and arms peddlers. Every ship, from a cooperating country, that enters any Hawaiian port has at least one of our observers on board. The police cooperate so that every plane that lands is scrutinized for shady characters. They pass the raw data to us because our analytical capabilities are superior to theirs. We in turn identify the known members of international underworld organizations."

"You see," Robert interjected, "our system is the most advanced in the world. No known undesirable character can avoid our surveillance. They can't move an inch without our knowing where. We never use violence or break any laws, but we have been known to physically escort known hit men to the airport and onto the plane."

"And, Robert went on, "there is only one exception to our policy. That is a drug dealer who is caught with the drugs in possession and is not put out of business by the authorities. If he returns to Honolulu in possession again, he is turned over to a group called, translated from Chinese, that is, the Vermin Exterminators. Somewhere at the bottom of the Pacific Ocean between Molokai and Maui there are quite a few former drug dealers who apparently caught their foot in an anchor and fell overboard."

"But, how do you get away with it?" Roy blurted out. "On the mainland every reporter, every liberal lawyer and do-gooder would tear your system to pieces. Your system gets the job done both efficiently and effectively. Mainland American liberals wouldn't allow it. It is too simple; it hurts the bad guys and helps the good guys."

Robert had sincere and strong convictions, "Professor, Hawaii is the only state with an oriental preponderance. Here we are pragmatic; we trust the honest citizens who come up with practical solutions. The police know that we are on their side and that we save them millions of tax dollars. We work together as a team to battle drugs and every other dishonest activity. On the mainland the news media perpetuates its own success by emphasizing racial and gender differences. After all, more friction creates more news stories. Here, we have every nationality and race you can imagine, but we emphasize cooperation and harmony."

"But, don't you get in trouble with the hard line on drug dealers?"

"Just think about it", Robert said, "what if a group of men could become millionaires by going around killing children. The parents of the children, instead of protecting them, deliberately make it difficult for their own law enforcement agencies to catch the killers. If they are caught, the parents pass laws that make it almost impossible to collect any convicting evidence, or to disallow it, if collected. If there is a trial, they pay for the expenses of the trial, and if convicted, which is rare, the parents make sure that the killers spend less than one year in jail."

Wouldn't any reasonable person think that the parents were crazy?

Robert went on, knowing that this was a rhetorical question. "That is a description of what the mainland Americans are doing. Drugs kill their children by the millions, and they are more concerned about the constitutional rights of the killers than about the lives of their own children."

Roy contemplated, "I have to admit, Robert, you have a point." George said, "getting back to your immediate problem, Professor Nelson, Robert asked me to trace any recent underworld movements on the Islands."

"In the past week, two members of the Japanese 'yakuza', code names, Amos and Andy, followed an abnormal movement pattern. They flew into Honolulu from San Francisco on Monday and checked into the Queen Kapiolani. On Tuesday morning, they drove out to Kahala and parked on Ocean Drive for an hour or so. Then they drove to King's Bakery for a late breakfast. After breakfast they drove to the Pali Lookout, stayed for only fifteen or twenty minutes and returned to the hotel. They remained there and had their meals at the restaurant in the hotel. On Wednesday morning they flew to San Francisco and our surveillance terminated."

Roy's heart was beating faster, he asked out of curiosity, "why is their pattern considered abnormal?"

George answered, "those two are killers, so they were watched every minute. They didn't seem to accomplish anything. Their phone calls were monitored, and they made no arrangements to do anything. That! my friend, is an abnormal pattern. Our computers are set to pinpoint irregular behavior."

Robert added, "The Japanese 'yakuza' is the epitome of efficiency. They do not send their best exterminators, and Amos and Andy are top of the line, out for tea parties. Our computers almost had a nervous break-down!"

Roy had to constrain himself, because he was tempted to give Robert and George the simple explanation for the abnormal behavior of Amos and Andy. He had no idea why the two 'yakuza' thugs pushed him over the Pali cliff, yet, it had to be. It was perfectly logical and he couldn't refute it. So, rather than speculate, he would wait for all the answers, before telling Robert and George.

"Robert, I know that they are now out of your range,

but, could you find out where they go from San Francisco?

"That's easy Professor Nelson, I will have it for you tonight. Shall I call you at the Royal Princess?"

"No, I think we'll go to George's Pagoda tonight. Would you please call me there. Oh, by the way, are there other members of the Japanese mafia, or 'yakuza', as you call it, active on the Island right now? I just wondered how they operate here in Hawaii?"

George handed Roy some copies of articles on the Japanese 'yakuza' which appeared in recent magazines and newspapers. He said. "These articles will tell you a little about the 'yakuza'. There is a man called Ito Takeda operating as a legitimate businessmen buying property in the industrial park. He has the title, Director, Japanese Global Trade Organization, representing several large Japanese companies which control the automotive parts industry. But, he appears on our list as connected with the Japanese 'yakuza'. There was no communication between Takeda and Amos and Andy while they were concurrently on the Island."

Good, Roy thought to himself, that means that his assailants would probably not find out for a while that their mission had failed. To be safe, he would not return to the Kahala house tonight; perhaps Luana would know where he might stay for the night. And then tomorrow he had better get back to Mackinaw and start to unravel this whole mess, if he could stay alive that long.

Roy thanked Robert and George and left the historic Wo Fat building. The streets around Wo Fat's were noted for their lei shops; Roy stopped at the corner shop and purchased two beautiful hand made leis. He had arranged to pick up Tamar and to meet Luana for dinner at the Pagoda Restaurant.

9

THE building was round, and built completely over a shallow man-made pond filled with what looked like giant goldfish, but were really carp. The Pagoda had been one of Roy's and Eleanor's favorite restaurants, especially for breakfast, as long as Roy could get a table by the water. He loved to watch the schools of multicolored fish swim in and out of the piers that supported the outside walls of the circular restaurant. To Roy the Pagoda was a tropical paradise just like the famous Willows Restaurant, where the thatched roof tables were so far apart that you couldn't even hear your neighbors talking.

The restaurant was not busy, so they were able to find an isolated table by the water. Tamar and Luana wore mumu's and together were the two most authentic looking Hawaiian wahine's and, in Roy's opinion, the two most beautiful women on the Island. Roy had managed to hide the leis in a department store bag. Before they were seated he placed a fresh lei over the head of each lady with the traditional kiss on the cheek.

Roy and Eleanor were not mouth kissers when it came to friends and relatives. Poor Eleanor shivered when she saw Roy's Uncle Heck come at her with his lips pursed for the big kiss. Eleanor was petite, while Uncle Heck was a burly railroad conductor with the Michigan Central; he almost squeezed her to death. He and his family were huggers and kissers. He was Roy's favorite uncle because he always had a sense of humor.

After the Pupu Platter, an appetizer with teriyaki baby spareribs, shrimp, skewered beef and chicken, Roy had the sauteed Mahi-Mahi and the ladies had a native Hawaiian dish with Poi. A tourist once described Poi to Roy and Eleanor as tasting like wallpaper paste. The description was quite accurate.

Luana was anxious to know what Robert found out for Roy. "I can't wait to hear about the meeting. Were they able to help?"

"Robert and his friend George actually isolated the two culprits who tried to kill me; they gave them the code names of Amos and Andy," Roy began. "They are members of the Japanese 'yakuza', which is their name for organized crime syndicates."

"But, why would they want to kill you, Roy?" Tamar didn't know what else to say. Roy had asked Luana to give her mother a sketch of what had happened, but not to worry her with all the details.

"I don't know, but it must have something to do with the murders of my two friends; and the Japanese mafia must think that I know something that is dangerous to their cause, whatever that may be. I'm leaving tomorrow for Mackinaw Village to try to figure out this puzzle. In the meantime, I don't want to stay at the Kahala house because I don't want them to know that I'm still alive. According to George, they will probably think that they succeeded in killing me, at least until I return to Mackinaw, where I can protect myself."

Luana frowned, "aren't you safer here, with Robert to protect you? Wouldn't you feel better, Mother, if Professor Nelson stayed here for a while longer, instead of taking a chance back in Michigan?"

Roy didn't even recognize Luana's clever pressure tactic; but he explained before Tamar could support her daughter, "I have a neighbor, Clayton, who works for the Coast Guard; when he's off duty he loves to fish and hunt and enjoy the woods. He was a Marine and he can twist a bear in half with his bare hands, at least that's what he boasts! Another of my friends, Stanley, is nicknamed Paul Bunyan, so I will be safe back home."

Roy was exaggerating, perhaps to ease the concern of his two lady friends. Stanley was actually 72 years old, but he didn't have to mention that. Besides, Paul Bunyan was not a household name in Hawaii, and the significance of Roy's comment went right over Tamar's head.

Tamar said, "unlike Luana, I really don't know where you are safest, Roy, but, if you're not staying at the Kahala house tonight, there is plenty of room at my place and you are welcome to stay there."

"Mother, it's better for Professor Nelson to stay at my apartment. No matter how innocent we know it is, your gossipy neighbors will make assumptions as long as

Dad is not there."

"I'll stay here at the Pagoda," Roy insisted. "I don't want to impose on either one of you."

Luana had the last authoritative word, "you will stay at my place. Mother and I both know what a perfect gentleman you are, and you must be among friends on your last night here."

Luana invited her mother, her Uncle Simon and Aunt Lanea, and some cousins over to her apartment to remove any feeling of impropriety that Roy might have. Tamar and her relatives entertained with Hawaiian songs and hulas all evening. Luana had put on a short mumu, more like a sarong, for one of her fast hulas and left it on all evening.

Tamar and her relatives left, about eleven o'clock. The moment the door closed and Luana gave him a mischievous smile, Roy was struck with the realization that they were alone. During his entire life he had been a survivor, but to spend the night with this provocative beauty queen was a challenge that Roy had not anticipated.

Luana was beginning to sense an inexorable accumulation of concern for this man, who was, just a few days ago, as Roy had put it, almost a stranger. She found herself unconsciously wanting to tempt him with her sexual attributes, which she knew were fatal to ordinary men. But was this man ordinary?

She sprawled seductively on the couch, with her long black hair falling over her generous bosom and flowing along her slender tan legs. Roy sat in an old-fashioned rocking chair, which helped him to divert his attention and remain calm. Not that Roy would ever have any problem with self control; but his eyes, seeing her lying on the couch, sent seductive messages to his heart, which were intercepted by his brain. And that's what bothered him.

They just chatted for a while when Luana said, "I'm going with you."

"You are not; it is much too dangerous to be around me until this mystery is cleared up. I will not allow it." Roy recalled that he had just said, "I will not"... something, in that same definitive tone, and was subsequently overruled by Luana. This time he would not give in, Luana suspected; so she quickly compromised.

"Alright I'll wait two weeks. Then I'll take some vacation time off. I insist on helping you, and besides I have never been to Mackinaw and have always wanted to see the Island with no cars and the Grand Hotel. I've wanted to see it all my life."

She had offered Roy just enough of a delay so that he could say, "Yes, perhaps it will be safe to come after two weeks or so. However, if things get worse you'll have to wait until it's safe."

Luana was happy that Roy accepted the fact that she was, at some time, definitely going to Mackinaw. At least he didn't veto the idea altogether. Over the past few days she had come to know a real friend, someone she admired and respected, someone with compassion as well as a sense of humor; someone she enjoyed being with. She was afraid that the friendship would end when Roy went back to Mackinaw. She was desperately afraid that he would be killed.

Luana couldn't understand her feelings. It was as if love was trying to burst out of its shell and they were both taping up the cracks as they appeared. She was a perfect lady. He was a perfect gentleman. Neither would destroy the respectability of their relationship. Sexual love was out of the question, she assured herself; this was a friendship love; Freud would know how to explain it.

Luana drove Roy to the Honolulu Airport on Friday afternoon. She wore a navy blue and white flowered full length dressy mumu. Eleanor had told her once that it was Roy's favorite color combination, and she remembered, even though at the time it had been insignificant to her. She let her black hair flow loosely around her shoulders, and wore one dainty white lei, that lay respectfully over her chest.

Silent moments passed while Roy noticed every detail about her; he noticed that her eyes were brown; he noticed the exotic elegance of her face, and he couldn't get over how beautiful she looked in that dress, just like Eleanor. But, Roy was a master at containing his emotions, his conscious mind ignoring the potential eruption of feelings, that to him were unthinkable.

Luana was well aware of the significance of those moments of silence; she had mesmerized men before, and was pleased that even stubborn Roy was human. Luana broke the silence, "I'll see you in two weeks; at the Pellston airport. I'll call and let you know the flight number. Don't try and talk me out of it; and please be careful."

Roy said, "Luana, you and your mother mean a lot to me. It has been hard for me since Eleanor disappeared, and you two have helped me feel alive again. You were both good friends to Eleanor, and I want you to know how much I appreciate that friendship."

After his nice, but rather stuffy, speech he gave her a fatherly hug. "Oh, before I forget, would you please start calling me Roy."

"Finally," thought Luana, "he broke through the formality." She placed a lei of fresh flowers, made by Tamar, around his neck and kissed him gently on each cheek. Roy blushed and waved goodby before boarding the flight to Chicago and on to Pellston, Michigan.

•

Earlier that same day Tamar Kameha walked along the waters edge at Waimanalo Beach. The sun dropped out of sight abruptly sending a spontaneous chill into the air. Her body and soul responded immediately to the sun's obedience. She even knew where to look. She involuntarily stared at the dark clouds circling above Ulupau Crater at the Kaneohe Marine Air Corps Station.

She saw Madame Pele's face forming in the clouds. Oh, she knew Madame Pele was real all right. Although Tamar was not a pure Hawaiian, her high percentage of Hawaiian blood qualified her as one of the only 2,000 or so left. She never doubted Pele, even though her husband, Walter, not a purebred, and her daughter, Luana, called her silly and superstitious.

But this time Pele was smiling. Tamar had never seen her smile before in her whole life. She was usually angry, her face a distorted entanglement of light and dark clouds swirling into grotesque shapes. Either she was scolding, pointing a finger at Tamar, or she was disgusted, disappointed with her little wahine. Tamar's mother, Zelda, had told her, when she was a little girl, that Pele smiled only when she was about to get revenge.

Zelda Kalakaua was one of the most respected Tutu's on Oahu. She was the organizer of the Tutu's, mostly purebred grandmothers, who visited the grade schools to teach the children their Hawaiian culture and heritage, including the myths. She made her children and even her grandchildren learn the dances and the chants, and they also had to memorize the legend of Pele. Tamar could still remember every word.

"Pele, a daughter of Haumea the Earth Mother and Wakea the Sky Father, is the goddess of fire, the maker of mountains, melter of rocks, eater of forests, and burner of lands—creator and destroyer both in one. She appears among mortal men sometimes as a beautiful young woman, tempting them, oftener as a wrinkled old hag, testing them. Whatever form she takes, Pele is unpredictable and tempestuous, as only a proud and jealous female can be. She does not ask for love. She demands respect. Here you must "step lightly, for you are on holy ground," the Hawaiians said in days of old.

Pele came to the Hawaiian Islands long ago, in flight from a cruel older sister, the goddess of the sea, Na Maka o Kaha'i. Pele went first to Ni'ihau, making a crater home there with her digging stick. Na Maka broke into that shallow pit, forcing Pele to flee again. On Kaua'i she dug a greater house. Na Maka chased her away from there too.

And so the pursued Pele ran, from place to place, from O'ahu to Moloka'i, to Lana'i, and Maui, each in turn; and from each successive home, the unrelenting Na Maka drove her out. At length, weary of being so harried, Pele dug deep and built high on the Island of Hawai'i. Here, at last, in these huge fortress-mountains, she has found a refuge from Na Maka o Kaha'i, at least for a while."

Tamar was mystified by the Madame's rare smile. She couldn't help feeling that Pele had a secret that she was trying to reveal only to her. Because, even though the clouds were dispersing rapidly, Pele's face reappeared in whatever cloud formation that followed. And she continued smiling at Tamar. Then in an instant the face disappeared, and she knew that Pele wanted her to be part of the secret, the revenge, if that's what it was.

Was the revenge going to be against some tourist?

The tourists were told not to take one piece of lava rock from Madame Pele's home or something drastic would surely happen. Their plane would crash, or they would get a terminal illness. Tamar could tell many tragic stories of tourists who dared to challenge the powers of Pele.

Tamar would know Pele's secret soon enough, for she and her daughter, Luana, would be Madame Pele's instruments in carrying out her most clever plan. Pele had waited long enough, though just an instant to her, to get revenge for the unprovoked and dastardly bombing of the Hawaiian Islands. Pearl Harbor didn't bother Pele as much as the attack on Kaneohe, where they dared to bomb her precious Ulupau Crater, and if a tourist had to pay dearly for merely taking a single piece of lava rock from her, what must she have in store for the perpetrators of such devastation and destruction to her cherished home.

10

Roy had left his 98 Olds with his neighbor, Clayton LaCombe, who picked him up at the Pellston airport at noon on Saturday, June 27. In late June the weather was normally comfortable, but noticeably cooler after the consistent 80's of the Hawaiian Islands. During the fifteen mile drive to Mackinaw Village Roy explained the extraordinary events to Clayton, asking that he not mention a single word about it to anyone.

"You mean these yakoozy buggars tried to push you off a cliff? What were you doing at the edge of a cliff, anyway?"

"It's a tourist attraction; it's where King Kamehameha forced his enemies over the cliff and became the undisputed king of Hawaii. I love to go there because of the view."

"OK, but why would the Japanese mob want to kill you?"

"I haven't figured that out yet. There has to be some connection between the murders of Dr. Makinen and Harold Martin, and the attempt to kill me; I'm sure of it. Clayton, you are the only person, besides Luana, who knows everything about what has happened. I told you because I may need your help, but it may be dangerous. So don't hesitate to just say no."

Clayton, or the former Marine in him, was thrilled, "Are you kidding? Would I love to tear those mafiosos, or yakoozies, to pieces. Just let me at em! Let me at em!", he sputtered, imitating the cowardly lion.

Clayton LaCombe's ancestors were French Canadian fur traders; they helped the Indians fight the English in the Revolutionary War and the War of 1812. They settled in the Mackinac area in the 1880's. One of his great grandfathers married a Huron Indian. Clayton lived in a small cottage right next door to Roy. Roy felt a little more secure with him knowing the situation. He was in combat in Viet Nam for two years and returned home with no physical or emotional damage.

When Clayton was sixteen he was a boy scout. His scoutmaster was a former Green Beret who made the older scouts camp out in the woods during January in 20 below zero weather. He took them scuba diving in Lake Superior in the Spring when sane people wouldn't even put their little finger in the water. But, he taught them how to survive and it paid off for Clayton who took the Marine training in stride. The tough guys from the cities were amateurs compared to Clayton, and many of them owed their lives to his intuitive common sense during combat.

As soon as Roy got home he began experiencing the usual effects of jet lag. It wasn't the time difference as much as the fact that Roy could never sleep on the plane. So when he flew from Honolulu to Michigan, he was up half a day, then all night, and when he arrived in Michigan it was the next day. He was so tired that he slept until noon the following day. Roy wanted to keep a low profile, but he had to work fast or he might be in the obituaries before he even knew why. That bothered him.

"If I'm gonna be rubbed out, I wanna know why," he repeated out loud, imitating Jimmy Cagney.

He wandered around the cottage muttering to himself. He was trying to reconstruct the sequence of bizarre events, so that they would fit into some logical explanation.

First, Roy suspected right from the time he found out about the Finnish connection between Dr. Makinen and Harold Martin that those two children were involved. He remembered seeing a story about Eva Braun in an old issue of Life magazine that he and Eleanor had purchased from an antique store in Cheboygan.

"Where would it be?"

Eleanor had put the old magazines in a box and Roy stacked them in the garage, he remembered. He easily found a stack of several Life magazines from 1939 to 1946. Roy was fascinated by reading about the war years, and Life seemed to capture the people's point of view, with pictures and stories.

Finally he found it in the June 25, 1945 issue, which he noted, was 10 cents. There was a big picture of Eva Braun entitled, Mrs. Adolph Hitler, under which was printed:

"Eva Braun poses for a leggy, flatteringly soft-focused portrait, possibly by photographer Heinrich Hoffman through whom she met Hitler. The short article read: "The first good authentic photograph of Eva Helene Braun, the woman in Hitler's life, arrived in the U.S. last week. It was obtained from her sister by three correspondents, one of them...(a Life reporter). It reveals a dark blonde not averse to displaying shapely legs for a cheese-cake picture. Along with the photograph came startling news. Marshal Zhukov revealed that Russian detectives attempting to trace Hitler had found Nazi diaries which described how he and Eva Braun married 48 hours before the German capital fell. A Stockholm dispatch said that this had been done to legitimize a boy and girl, 5 and 4 respectively, whom Miss Braun had borne the Fuhrer..... Of special interest to hunters of Hitler was a half-burned letter found in his supersecret Berlin bombshelter. The letter ... in Eva Braun's handwriting... confided that she would disappear for a time."

Many historians cite evidence that Hitler committed suicide along with Eva Braun, but there was no mention of children. This story in Life indicates that there definitely were children, and that they completely disappeared. The Finnish connection made more and more sense.

The secret mission, which Dr. Makinen commanded, must have been to transport those children, who were perfectly innocent in the minds of any humane person, to a safe haven with a new identity. The children could have been secretly taken to Finland in order to be evacuated as war refugees to the United States or possibly to Canada.

In 1945, the boy in the picture was five and the girl

was four. The boy would now be 51 or 52 and the girl would be one year younger. So the two children of Adolph Hitler could be leading a normal life almost anywhere in the world with completely new identities. They could be in the United States, they could be in Michigan right now, and no one would know their true identity.

Second, Dr. Makinen and Harold were the only two remaining witnesses to the transporting of the woman and the children. Harold is dead and Dr. Makinen is presumed dead. The conclusion is that someone or some organization does not want the whereabouts of those children known. And their reason is powerful enough to kill anyone who may expose them.

Third, Dr. Makinen must have said or done something at the Grand Hotel that fateful night, which indicated that he knew something.

Fourth, the letter to Harold was found by someone who assumed that he also knew about the children, either who they are or where they are.

Fifth, and this is not clear at all, the Japanese Mafia, the 'yakuza', are involved in some way. It is possible that they are disturbed about my research and articles exposing the Japanese marketing strategy in the American auto parts industry. If the 'yakuza' are attempting to capture the U.S. auto parts market they might consider me a threat to their success. And I have been the most outspoken academic critic of the collaborative activities of the major Japanese auto assemblers and their suppliers. But, that is far fetched, because many researchers have been publishing articles criticizing the Japanese tactics; and stopping me would be insignificant in the overall economic picture.

It is more likely that they think I know something about the Makinen and Martin connection. They might assume that because I happened to travel from Mackinaw to Honolulu, and because I happen to know both men, that I must be involved. But, that still doesn't explain why the Japanese 'yakuza' are involved." Roy had neatly outlined the events. Now it was time to interpret the events and to take action. The piece of paper in Dr. Makinen's car, it said, Raymond Hansler, 1940. Governor Raymond Hansler, could it mean that he was born in 1940? Could it mean that he was the boy? No wonder someone doesn't want the world to find out. He was just named as a possible Vice-Presidential candidate by no other than President Barnes himself.

Roy had earlier purchased the Detroit News-Free press from the grocery store downtown. He remembered that an article in the business section said, "Governor to entertain visiting Japanese businessman, Ito Takeda, on Thursday at the Capitol. He will then entertain him at the Governor's Summer Residence on Mackinac Island on Friday." The article indicated that Mr. Takeda was Director of a Japanese Global Trade Organization which represented three major automotive supplier companies with plans to build plants in Michigan. Michigan suppliers were opposed to any concessions by the Governor.

Roy's research revealed that there was a clearly defined marketing strategy being followed by the Japanese auto transplants and their suppliers. In the State of Michigan, the top 21 auto suppliers were reported to be showing net losses, beginning in about 1990. The major Japanese-owned auto assembly plants were buying only Japanese-made parts. When they were pressured to buy from U.S. plants, they rapidly built supplier plants around the assembly plants and claimed that the parts were made in America. Roy's interviews of Japanese-owned supplier's revealed clearly that they were receiving 50% to over 90% of their materials from Japan already in assembled form. The U.S. plant merely added a few screws, placed the parts in a box and shipped them off to the Honda or the Toyota plant. The Japanese were systematically squeezing the U.S.-owned auto supplier plants out of business.

The proof was in a case study, which was the basis for an article that Roy submitted and was published by one of the Michigan university journals. A Japanese-American joint-venture in an "Auto Alley" state operated in the red for four years. Its prices were set by the Japanese-owned assembler in Ohio. The prices were so low that no American firm could compete. Because the losses were too heavy for the American firm in the joint-venture it had to sell all but 5% to the Japanese owner. Immediately after the sale the Japanese firm raised the prices on the parts it purchased and the joint-venture made profit in the fifth year. The marketing strategy is that the Japanese assemblers and suppliers collaborate in order to eliminate competition. The U.S. assemblers have no loyalty to U.S. suppliers. Our laws do not permit collaboration among U.S. firms, but they allow Japanese firms to operate with impunity.

Roy hadn't yet figured out how, or if, there was any connection between the news story and the other events. He must find out what the meeting between Governor Hansler and Takeda was all about. Then he remembered that George said that Takeda was in some way connected with the Japanese 'yakuza'. Was there a connection between him and the two men who Roy assumed had pushed him over the Pali cliff? George had said that there was no communication between them in Honolulu. But that was standard procedure anyway. Their missions could still be connected.

Roy must find out where Takeda and Amos and Andy

flew to after they left Honolulu. Either Robert forgot to call him at the Pagoda last Thursday night, or he didn't have any information yet. He was supposed to find out where the two hit-men were going.

Roy called Robert at the restaurant on Monday. He knew that Robert always manned the register during the day, and it would be Monday noon in Honolulu. Robert answered, and after the formalities of identification, Roy asked, "Did you find out where Amos and Andy were headed?"

"Yes and no, Professor Nelson; they had tickets to San Francisco. They were monitored right up to the security gates, however, we later found out that they did not board the plane. They evaded our system at that point. Takeda has tickets through Chicago to Lansing, Michigan on Wednesday afternoon. We will make sure that he actually gets on the plane."

Robert added, "Now, this may be something to watch. There is a Japanese registered freighter, the Fujima, which left Honolulu three hours after the plane was scheduled to leave. The Fujima will be traveling through the St. Lawrence Seaway on its way to Chicago. It will pass the Mackinac Bridge about the thirteenth or fourteenth of July."

"Our two culprits could have boarded that ship since the present owners of the Fujima do not cooperate with us. They know how we operate because we invited the former owners to join in our information system before they sold out to a Japanese 'yakuza'-owned company. So they could have pre-planned the departure procedure of the two hit men in order to avoid our monitoring system. If so, they have gone to a lot of trouble. They must be on a highly sensitive mission. Does this make any sense?"

"It sure does, thank you again Robert, you have been

a great help. I'll stop in to thank you personally as soon as I return to Honolulu."

Roy was careful not to show any emotion, even though he was deeply concerned with this last bit of news. It was clear now that the 'yakuza' was involved. The next step for him was to find out what their mission was, and to stay alive doing it.

He did not want Robert and his friends to get embroiled any further in the mess until he knew more about what was happening. On the other hand, they provided him with the only possible avenue for this kind of information, and they seemed to be quite capable of taking care of their own interests, to say the least.

11

ROY remained inconspicuous until Friday. He called Clayton, "I am going over to Mackinac Island tonight to try to find out something, do you want to come with me?

"Are you kidding, I wouldn't miss it for the world. Would I love to wipe up the floor with those crooks."

"No, no! This is strictly undercover. The Governor is entertaining this Takeda fellow at the Governor's Mansion tonight. I'm hoping that you and I can get close enough to find out what relationship there is between Takeda and Governor Hansler. There are just too many coincidences; there has to be a connection between Professor Makinen's disappearance, the Governor and Takeda, who is part of the 'yakuza'."

Roy knew that there was no heavy duty security protection on the Island. After all, there is virtually no crime there, and there are no cars on the Island, thus no getaways. Picture the bad guy racing away on his Schwinn or on his Clydesdale. Also, tourists walked all around the Governor's Mansion; they even had special tours inside when the building was not in use.

Clayton and Roy left on Clayton's boat. It was a 35 foot 1953 Chris Craft cruiser, named the Nicolet, which he displayed at the Les Cheneaux Islands Antique Wooden Boat Show in Hessel each August. Clayton had built his own dock and boat shelter in front of his cottage. During the Winters he babied it until it was in perfect condition each season. He always won some prize at the show.

They rented a space in the Mackinac Island Marina, docked the boat and went to the Dockside Inn for a snack. The Dockside was a favorite drinking place of the locals, and they had good food, a definition of Roy's, which meant that he liked their fresh fish entrees, lake whitefish, perch, trout, and walleye. Clayton loved his beer and Roy was amazed how it never seemed to have any noticeable effect on him. They had to kill some time because during June and July the sky was still partially illuminated by the sun's reflection until after 9:00 o'clock.

At dusk, they walked up the steep hill next to the fort, which led to Huron Road and the Governor's Mansion. They tried to look like tourists taking an evening stroll. The Governor's Mansion was built in 1901 and was a beautiful old structure. It was purchased by the State of Michigan in 1945 and became officially called the

Governor's Summer Residence. Mansion was not really the correct word for any of the Island houses. The hill houses were elegant and proud looking, but not massive.

During the late 80's their owners spruced them with new porches and paint. It gave them new life, almost as if the houses themselves could tell stories of their historical past and their former inhabitants to the tourists. The owner of the house next to the Grand Hotel let couples have their wedding ceremony in his gazebo on the expansive lawn.

Governor Hansler had told the state policeman and the pilot, who flew him and Ito Takeda to the 3,500 foot landing strip on the Island, to take a break. He didn't want anyone around during his discussions with Takeda. The two men walked downtown to the Pub, another popular restaurant on the Island.

Roy didn't know how lucky he was that night. The circumstances were perfect for Clayton and him to sneak in close to the house. It was fortunately a warm night, so the windows were open and Roy was able to overhear some of the discussion. Clayton stayed back fifty feet in the bushes to watch for trouble.

Mr. Takeda was speaking, in perfect English, "Governor, you have no choice; you must remove all opposition to the plants and assure us that the property tax concessions are made. We will give you until September 1 to clear the legal requirements."

Governor Hansler's voice lost some of its authoritative quality he was noted for as he responded, "You're asking the impossible; I'll need at least six months, maybe a year to get through the political opposition and the legal paperwork."

"Well then, we will have to tell the reporters about our little secret."

Before the Governor could reply, the housekeeper, Hilda, marched briskly down the ornate staircase and into the meeting room.

"A pleasure to see you again, Fraulein Schwartz," Takeda politely said. "Perhaps you can persuade your brother to comply with our gentlemen's agreement. The distinguished corporate leaders I represent gave their word, and they expect no less from Governor Hansler."

Roy knew from his research that the Japanese executives depend on verbal agreements among themselves. Their word is as good as a written contract. They do not take it lightly if that word is broken. It sounded as if the Governor had committed himself to the Japanese group.

Then it struck Roy that the Governor has a sister, perhaps one or two years younger than he. She was an unattractive, large boned, muscular woman. She wore a stylish, expensive looking dress to minimize her paucity of feminine features.

The Governor, Takeda and Hilda went into another room and closed the door. Roy couldn't hear anything else from his position. He walked cautiously around the house but was unable to hear any more talking.

Then Clayton warned, "there are two men coming up the hill, they are both in uniform."

Roy crouched down and retreated from the house to join Clayton. They climbed down the bank in front of the Governor's Residence to Turkey Hill Road and reached the tourist walkway without being seen. They walked through Marquette Park to the dock, jumped into the Nicolet, and cast off for Mackinaw Village.

"Thanks for going with me, Clayton, I couldn't have done it without your help."

"But, I didn't do anything except keep you company. I would have preferred a good fight. Why couldn't we just barge in and beat the hell out of those yakoozy buggars."

"They weren't even there; this was strictly politics. But I learned a lot tonight, and there is much more to this than we ever imagined. It's late, so lets relax on the way back, and I'll tell you everything in the morning."

Roy slept late on Saturday morning, it was the Fourth of July. His mind had been going a mile a minute all night as he tried to put all the pieces together. He remembered that Governor Hansler was a bachelor, but he had never read anything about a sister. They must have kept it low key. Takeda was threatening to expose him to the press for something, and the sister knew all about it.

"It fits, it fits," he almost shouted to himself. "Everything makes sense if Governor Hansler and his sister are Eva Braun and Hitler's children."

It was too early in Honolulu to call Robert so he waited until 3:00 in the afternoon.

"Hello Robert, will you do another favor for me. Can you find out, from someone who was in the Japanese high command during WWII, what they knew about Hitler and his family during the fall of the Nazi's in 1945?"

"Your questions are getting harder, Professor, but there is a man in his 80's, Tom Kita who, believe it or not, likes Chinese food. Our records show that he was Admiral Tomatsu Kita, who was promoted late in the war to replace the numerous losses they had in battle. He is a loyal American now, and he doesn't want to advertise his past, so we have some leverage with him. I'll get back with you tomorrow if possible."

Roy was awed by Robert's speed. He recalled that when he had changed his insurance coverage with the University's group plan a few years back, they accidentally removed Eleanor from the computer. It took six month's and scads of long distance calls to get her back on. Roy was convinced that the large corporations as well as the cumbersome public institutions in the U.S. had reached their highest point of inefficiency, and it worried him.

The next day, on Sunday, Robert called.

"I talked to Admiral Kita myself to assure him of his privacy; he said that the Japanese Secret Police assigned to Berlin knew everything that went on in Hitler's inner circle. During the chaos of the last days they had access to both Hitler's and the Nazi Regime's most secret records. Kita himself had seen the boxes of records that the Secret Police had retrieved before the Russians came, and when the Germans were too busy running for their lives to object.

The Russians took everything from Hitler's bunker when they arrived before the Americans. Stalin wouldn't cooperate with the Allies, and had all the records destroyed, so the world will never know what really happened. Admiral Kita claims that the Japanese records were subsequently stolen. It had to be someone with security clearance, but the records were so unimportant to the government that the investigation was dropped. They still have no idea who stole the records or why, and no one seems to care.

If you want more specific details Admiral Kita says that there is a former WWII Japanese officer residing in Honolulu who was there during the exodus. But, he is an American citizen now and doesn't want to reveal his name unless it is necessary."

"I don't think so, right now, but I'll let you know if I do, and Robert, I can't thank you enough for your help. I'm getting closer to solving the mystery, but... well, I'll tell you the whole story when I get all the answers. Right now I'd just be speculating. So long for now."

That evening, Roy read the articles that Robert had given to him about the Japanese 'yakuza'. The 'yakuza' consisted of crime families, similar to the mafia in the U.S. The Kobe-based Yamaguchi-gumi, Japan's largest crime family, is reported to have some 26,000 members. As the money rolls in from prostitution, drug trafficking, and extortion, the 'yakuza' has become more active in buying legitimate businesses as fronts. Japanese stock market traders estimate that there was the equivalent of three to four billion U.S. dollars of 'yakuza' money in the market by late 1991. The Japanese stock market scandal, involving the top executives of Nomura Securities Co. and Nikko Securities Co. was a direct result of 'yakuza' influence and interference.

Then Roy noted that in one of the articles it said that the 'yakuza' were expanding overseas, in particular to the U.S., and that prosecutors in Hawaii and in California had established special units to deal with them. The 'yakuza' money is aimed at legitimate investments in land, golf courses and stock.

12

Roy knew that he must verify the Governor and his sister's background. He called Martha Reed in Lansing. Martha was Roy's next door neighbor when they were growing up in Detroit. They went through all twelve grades together. She was always first, and Roy was always second in every spelling bee during their grade school days. Both were only children, so they had been just like brother and sister. She was such a brain that she became head of the State Statistical Records Department in Lansing. Roy observed that she had become more attractive than she had been as a child. Roy assumed that she had never married because she always had her nose in a book, and just wasn't the romantic type.

He drove down to Lansing on Monday morning, arriving at 11 o'clock. Martha met him in her spacious office, decorated to match her personality. He gave her a hug and Martha expressed her sorrow.

"I'm writing a book, Marty", he explained, "so I need to know about the childhood of Governor Hansler. This is not political so I'm not looking for anything scandalous, just whatever is public information. And, this may be a little more difficult, I would like you to try to locate a family named Schwartz, with an adopted daughter, who would have been a refugee from Europe after WWII."

"Is that all?" Martha scolded, "you sure expect a lot from your old pal. Does that mean you are taking me out to lunch!" Roy knew it was not a question. Martha gave specific instructions to a bespeckled subordinate.

"Byron is a whiz on the computer, he'll have whatever is available by the time we return from our expensive two-hour lunch," she teased.

Roy and Martha went to Pistachio's in East Lansing, it was their mutual choice for maximizing the combination of food, atmosphere and price. Martha was a career woman, completely satisfied with her lifestyle. She had a secret crush on Roy for a while when they were kids, even though he was considered masculine, but not 'cute', by most of the girls. Now, she couldn't help but notice that Roy looked rather distinguished, a few grey hairs from the the aging process had made him better looking.

When they returned to Martha's office, Byron was waiting with his 'hot off the press' information.

"Leave it here, Byron; if I have any questions I'll call

you in," Martha said, very businesslike. Roy was impressed.

"Ok, it looks as if the Governor was a five-year old war refugee adopted in 1945 by a Mr. and Mrs. Eric Hansler of West side Detroit, not far from where we lived, Roy. He went all through high school in Detroit and graduated from Wayne State University in 1962. He later went to Michigan State University for an MBA, graduating in 1975. Nothing unusual so far. His parents both died in an automobile accident just before he was elected Governor, in 1984. Wait, this is strange! They were hit head on by a semi truck at night on a lonely two lane highway near Lansing. And... listen to this, the truck was stolen and the driver was never found."

Martha continued, "now as to the Schwartz question, there is an Emil Schwartz, who was a prisoner of war in a Canadian work farm. His wife and a little girl, born in 1941, who was not their daughter, but was a war refugee, joined him in 1945. At the end of the war in Europe, Emil and his family were allowed to move to Detroit and they all became citizens. Not really so unusual when you consider the upheaval of people in the 1940's."

"Not at all," Roy tried to be as nonchalant as possible. "You have been a great help, Marty, you have restored my faith in good old American institutions."

"Please, and this is a command," said Martha as Roy got up to leave, "come down just to have lunch with me again, and it's my turn to treat you. You know you're just like a brother to me."

"I know, and I feel the same about you; I promise." They hugged and Roy took off in his Olds 98 for his favorite place, Mackinaw. He arrived at the cottage a little after eight p.m. The weather had been rather cool so far this Summer. It was a clear night and the water in the Straits was calm. The multi-colored lights on the bridge reflected off the mirror-like surface almost to the shoreline.

At Tuesday noon, Roy received a phone call from Martha.

"Byron came up with some interesting data on the Schwartz family. On July 9, 1978 there was a rally in Chicago's Marquette Park sponsored by the Nationalist Socialist Party of America, a white supremacist organization based on Adolph Hitler's Nazi Party. More than 2,000 demonstrators were milling around shouting racial slurs and Nazi slogans. A Supreme Court ruling a month earlier had been rendered giving them the right to demonstrate peaceably. It took 400 police officers to avert a riot between the Nazis and the counter-demonstrators. Listed among the leaders of the Nazi demonstrators were an Emil Schwartz and his daughter, Hilda. Byron also found out that Emil and his wife are both dead, but there is absolutely no more information on Hilda. That just means that she hasn't been arrested or done anything newsworthy. We don't attempt to nose around in anyone's private lives in this department."

"Believe it or not, Martha, that is more than I expected and exactly what I needed to know. Thank you for calling, I'll keep in touch."

Roy called Paul Tamber, "could you find out about everyone involved in the care and operation of the Governor's Mansion on the Island, and see if there is any kind of a schedule or routine that they follow. I am writing a book and need to understand the way they operate."

Paul knew that Roy was always researching something so he didn't question his motives.

"By the way," Paul asked, "what's new on the Makinen case. I know that you were never convinced that it was an accident."

"It's long story, Paul, and it's not over, yet. I'll tell you more if and when I can figure it out."

Roy did not want to involve anyone else until it became necessary. It was too bizarre of a story to convince anyone without proof, anyway.

•

In Lansing, Governor Hansler had called a meeting with three of his party's most influential state senators, Will Kent from the Flint area, Ralph Mankiewicz from Detroit, and Larry Trump, from Lansing.

"We must make the concessions if we want to stop this recession. It will mean an estimated two-thousand new jobs," the Governor was arguing.

Senator Kent fumed, "that's a lot of baloney, and you know it, Ray. Every one job that a Japanese-owned company creates in Michigan results in the elimination of two jobs in American-owned plants. They merely put up an assembly plant here and make all the parts in Japan.

Professor Nelson's article based on his case studies demonstrates exactly how they were able to circumvent all the superficial regulations. Some 70% to 80% of all parts that would be assembled in these new plants come either directly from Japan or are passed through a joint venture with token U.S. ownership. The new jobs are created in Japan and the U.S. auto industry gradually diminishes. Every major producer in the nation has announced employment cuts."

Senator Mankiewicz chimed in, "and the proof is in

the figures. Japan has too many jobs, an actual scarcity of workers, while the U.S. and Canada are displacing production workers by the thousands. When is the American public going to wake up. The Japanese are not to blame; it is our fault for letting them get away with it."

"But, I'm in the middle, "the Governor insisted, "if I fail to support these plants the public will blame me for the loss of jobs. They don't listen to the professors and their research, they listen to the media which quotes any statistic which proves their point. You can find a statistic to prove any position you want to take. They are masters at that game. Right now they are promoting these plants as new employment. It would be political suicide for me to oppose them."

Senator Trump agreed, "if Ray doesn't push hard for the concessions he will look bad in the eyes of our constituency. And don't forget the important factor that a Michigan Governor may be the next Vice-President. Ray's record has to be impervious to Democratic scrutiny. If he is associated with any action to lose American jobs it would be political suicide in this election."

Mankiewicz chimed in again, "I realize the importance of having Ray in the White House, but I'm concerned more for our state. I don't believe that the Federal legislators realize the importance of the automobile industry. The high middle class standard of living exists because of our automobile industry. The auto workers in Detroit, Flint and Lansing have been the highest paid factory workers in the world. They are being downgraded from a job paying 40 or 50 thousand dollars to a minimum wage job at K-Mart or Burger King. The collapse of the Big Three dominance will eventually lead to a lower standard of living throughout America, and what most Americans don't realize is that almost every industry will be affected."

The meeting ended with no consensus. Governor Hansler was noticeably concerned. He really agreed with his conservative friends, but he had more than one reason to support the Japanese lobby.

13

On Wednesday, Paul Tamber called, "Professor, this is Paul, I found out that the state provides a minimum of help at the Governor's Summer Residence. The resident housekeeper is a Hilda Schwartz, and the gardener is named William Smith; they are there all Summer until the end of the season. She does all the cooking and housework, and naturally he takes care of the grounds and maintenance. They sometimes need additional help when the Governor has guests. Security is provided by this Smith guy, who acts as a personal bodyguard, and by the State

Police, who sometimes, but not always, accompany the Governor to the Island. There's not much need for a bodyguard on Mackinac Island. There's been only one known murder in the 300 year history of the Island."

"Good work, thanks Paul; I'll call you if I need anything else."

The phone rang Wednesday afternoon at the cottage. Roy picked it up and Luana's voice said, "Professor Nelson, my plane will land in Pellston at noon on Friday. Do you need a flight number? The airline is called United Express and it will come from Chicago."

"Luana, you mustn't come yet; there is still danger. I haven't cleared this mystery up yet, and I don't want you to get hurt. Your mother would never forgive me."

"Professor, can I expect you to pick me up? This is my vacation, if you won't let me stay at your cottage I will get a motel room." Luana left no room for resistance; she was determined. She anticipated that Roy would continue to delay until something drastic might happen, so she took a firm approach hoping that he would acquiesce.

Roy had no choice, "No Luana, I mean yes, of course I will be there on Friday and you will stay at the cottage. I have a guest room for you. It's small, but it has a view of the Mackinac Bridge, from end to end. I think you'll like it. Don't forget to bring something warm, like a sweater or a warm robe, or both. It's cool in the Summer here and you aren't used to it."

"That's more like it," she thought.

"Are you sure that you won't be embarrassed about my staying at your place... you know what I mean. Would your friends think... well." Luana had difficulty in spitting it out. She knew that she had already secured her acceptance by Roy, but she wanted to let him know that she would understand his concern about what other people might think about him.

Roy sensed her meaning and assured her, "My close friends know me well, Luana, and the neighbors here aren't nosy. So don't worry about it. Besides, as of right now, I am Sherlock Nelson, private eye, and you are my chief investigator, Luana Watson. I need you here to investigate the case of the murder at Mackinac. The cottage will be our office; so, we both sleep at the office. What could be more innocent! By the way, didn't we agree that you would call me Roy."

Luana found it hard to call him Roy, "Thank you, Profes..., I mean, Roy, I can't wait to see Michigan and to start working." She really meant that she could hardly wait to see him, but she wouldn't dare say it.

The Pellston Airport was about as small as airports can be. There was no need for gate numbers, unless you wanted to call it Gate One. The airport has a small restaurant, some quarter gulpers, Roy's name for the electronic games, and one central waiting room. Deplaning passengers entered through a large door in the center of the building directly into the waiting area.

The flight was twenty minutes late as usual, but it gave Roy time to chat with his new neighbors, the Johnsons, who were waiting for their son, Kirk, to arrive. The Johnsons, who were friends of the Makinens in Ann Arbor, bought the cottage from Mrs. Makinen. The exchange took place while Roy was teaching in Hawaii. Clayton had told him about it.

Roy made it a point to introduce himself and to welcome the Johnsons, who seemed to be as delightful as the Makinens. When Kirk arrived, his parents seemed so pleased to see him, like a little boy coming home. Roy knew the feeling, your children are always your children, no matter how old they are. It is the most unselfishly, satisfying attachment there is among humans.

He couldn't help but think of his three boys, how he missed them after they grew up and became independent.

When Luana entered through the center doors, more than one pair of masculine eyes were pulled, magnetically, toward her. Luana wore a bright brown and white flowered mumu with several leis made of fresh multicolored orchids around her neck. She had white flowers in her straight black hair, so squeaky clean that it almost floated as she walked. Roy was almost afraid to look at her feet, expecting her to be barefoot. But, to his relief she wore sandals.

The light golden-brown skin of the former Miss Honolulu against the colorful background of her mumu was breathtaking, like an exotic Polynesian Goddess. Her appearance in that mundane little landing field among the sloppily dressed tourists would have been more believable had she swooped down from the clouds on wings. Roy gained back his composure just in time to give Luana his fatherly hug. He placed his head over her right shoulder, his two arms around her shoulders, and gave a little squeeze to transmit his protective, paternal welcome. "Luana, welcome to Michigan. It's good to see you; you look so... so!"

Luana's Polynesian breeding, along with the emotional impact of seeing Roy, overruled her sense of propriety. The conditioning of years of dancing the slow Hawaiian hula encouraged her soft body to ooze into all the empty spaces between them. Each segment of her voluptuous figure pressed firmly against Roy's body sending a message of seduction far exceeding the most explicit love scene imaginable. As Roy slowly drew his head back from Luana's shoulder, their lips almost touched as they looked into each other's eyes. It was a moment suspended in time; so precious that they both desperately wanted it to last until eternity. But each knew the reality of the moment; it was a spontaneous embrace unauthorized by their relationship.

Roy quickly snapped out of the trance and stumbled back. "Umm, well, you must have some luggage; it comes out over here," he pointed to the rental car desk...."I mean over there." He, still in a daze, led her to the small room at the back of the airport where luggage lumbered around and around until someone heisted it off the circular conveyor.

Luana felt a little devilish. She had deliberately tempted poor Roy when she knew full well what effect she had on men. She had that indefinable exotic allure in her face and thoughout her whole body. The shape of her mouth when she smiled and the sensual movement of her brown eyes set in the bronze skin of her cheeks were irresistible to men.

Although she couldn't quite understand it, she had watched men make absolute idiots of themselves over her. In her younger, Miss Honolulu days, men had offered her apartments, jewelry, money, cars, almost anything for her affection. Thanks to Tamar, she had self respect and moral principles that had no price.

"There they are," Luana pointed to two large blue suitcases.

Roy put them in the trunk of his trusty Olds 98, and they drove toward Mackinaw Village. There was an extraordinary silence for the first five miles as thoughts were prevailing over tongue.

Roy was deeply concerned with the electrifying impulses that had gone through his body. Only once before had it happened. Eleanor's cousin and Roy's best friend had a date for New Year's Eve. They arranged for Roy and Eleanor to double-date with them. They went to the enormous Grande Ballroom on Grand River Avenue in

Detroit. In those days, alcoholic beverages were not allowed in a public ballroom, so everybody had a fun time. There were no obnoxious drunks, no fights, and no electronic noise blasters. At midnight, the band played Auld Lang Syne and everyone kissed. Roy and Eleanor were virtually strangers and both were timid, but they were also embarrassed to just stand there. So Roy gently kissed her soft lips, and what started as a perfunctory duty was quickly converted into ecstatic impulses flowing through his entire body. They both claimed unequivocally that they fell in love with that kiss. During the next slow dance to 'Moonglow', Roy bravely put his arm around her waist and pulled her tightly to him.

Luana was a little mad at herself. She wanted to maintain a respectable relationship with Roy. She wanted him to fall in love with her, not her appearance. She had learned that she could attract just about any unattached man with her outward appearance. Roy was the first man she met who could distinguish between love and sexual attraction. Playing games with him might destroy the purity of their affection toward one another. And until Roy was convinced that Eleanor was dead, there would be no chance for her or anyone else.

Luana fumbled with words, "I'm sorry, ... I didn't mean to... I guess I was so happy to see you that.... well... "

Roy, equally embarrassed, pulled her out of her dilemma, "Well Luana, can you believe that you are finally in Mackinaw? There it is, there's the bridge."

It was a clear day. There it was, the proud Mackinac Bridge in its majestic splendor stretched out to join the two Michigan peninsulas. Luana, who was native to the most beautiful ocean waters in the world, the green, lush mountains, the awesome craters, tropical birds of every shape, size and color, and the indescribable attractions of the Hawaiian paradise, was thrilled.

Roy drove down the waterfront. The ferry boats were taking off every fifteen minutes for Mackinac Island. Both locals and tourists were fishing for perch off the municipal dock. The main street was filled with 'fudgies', as the tourists were called. The wives were in the shops buying fudge, while some of the men preferred to wait outside and watch or chat with the other 'fudgies'.

As they arrived at the quaint, yellow cottage, the temperature had already dropped from the 75 degrees at Pellston to 65 by the water. Luana was shivering and Roy tenderly put the sweater he always kept in the car around her shoulders.

"What a beautiful cottage," she smiled. She examined every room and when she saw the sweeping view from the front porch she felt a nostalgic dejavu. She had frequently visited her Tutu, who lived near Tamar in Waimanalo. She lived in a small yellow, oceanfront house which was built on stilts.

In spite of her happy excitement, she couldn't stop shivering. Roy knew the reaction. When he lived in Florida he and Eleanor visited friends in Detroit for a few days, and he shivered for several hours before his body adjusted to the change in climate.

And Luana's body had never experienced the coolness of the Northern climate. She lay down on the couch and Roy covered her with a warm blanket. He helped her take off the leis and the flowers in her hair. He heated some water for tea, but by the time it was ready she was sound asleep. She had been awake for some twenty-two hours. Roy looked down at her and gently ran his hand through her hair and touched her cheek. He and Eleanor had three boys, but no girls. He never admitted it to anyone, but he would have liked a soft, cuddly little girl.

Luana slept until Saturday afternoon. When she seemed recovered from the jet lag Roy drove her downtown to the Mackinaw Clothing Company, where, at Roy's insistence, she picked out a lightweight denim jumper and a long-sleeved blouse. Her clothes were just too flimsy for the cooler temperatures.

As they returned to the cottage, Roy spotted Clayton next door and called him over to meet Luana. Clayton was obviously stunned by Luana's beauty, even though she was wearing her new northern outfit and had piled her flowing hair on top of her head in some kind of a bun. He had no social restraint and his approval of her physical attributes was too obvious. Clayton was not only known as a rugged, muscular man; he also had the reputation of being a ladies man. Luana found him attractive and liked his sincere friendliness.

"Clayton has worked with me on the case and knows what has happened so far," Roy was explaining to Luana. He also had to update her on the events of the past two weeks. Roy was beginning to see the three of them as a team working together to solve the mystery which started on May 14 with the disappearance of Professor Makinen on the Mackinac Bridge.

Clayton lured Roy over to his place, next door, with some excuse to express his rather colorful enthusiasm, "Roy, I can't get over you shackin up with that gorgeous piece of ..."

Roy abruptly interrupted, "Clayton, Luana is the daughter of a good friend of mine and Eleanor's. She is merely staying at my cottage for convenience, just as I stayed at her place in Honolulu. I have absolutely no... no personal relationship with her of the type that you have in mind. And she thinks of me as well,... perhaps as a friend of her mother." Roy was a master at beating around the bush with the English language, not untypical of college professors.

"You did, that is, you stayed at her place in Honolulu?"

"Well... yes, but only after it was too dangerous to stay at the Martin's place, and she has a guest room, just as I do. We're friends, that's all, and no more. In fact, she wants to help us because she's just as fascinated as we are over this mystery."

Then Roy shot a facetious question at Clayton, "you don't mind her working with us do you?"

Clayton looked at Roy with a silly smirk, "well, as long as you're not interested, it'll be an inconvenience, but, I'll manage to put up with her."

"Now look Clayton, you must treat her as a lady. She's not one of your one night stands. She's a decent girl... she's... "

This time Clayton cut Roy off with a laugh, "OK, daddy, I'll be good to your little girl."

Roy punched him on the shoulder and they tumbled into an arm wrestle, Clayton winning, but not without a struggle. Roy was a solid contender at the arm wrestle, but nobody in town could beat Clayton LaCombe.

•

That night, the TV networks announced that President Barnes was going to select a new running mate. The incumbent Vice-President had been consistent in embarrassing the president with his spontaneous, controversial remarks, the kind that the other party dreams about for future political quotes. The party leaders pressured the Vice-President to make up some excuse not to run again. After his announcement of withdrawal, the party spokesman named Governor Hansler along with a few others as likely choices. The selection was expected to be made in one week at the Republican National Convention.

•

On Sunday Roy and Luana went to church services at the small Bible Church in Mackinaw Village. It reminded Luana of the Waimanalo Hawaiian Church her family attended. After church they drove the sixty miles to Sault Ste. Marie, stopping at Rudyard to pick up some 'squeaky cheese' at the Finnish Dairy.

During the early years of their marriage Roy and Eleanor had frequently visited her Aunt Bessie, who lived on farm near Escanaba in the Upper Peninsula. She, like most of the older generation Scandinavians, made Finnish cheese from a 'starter' and Roy just loved to listen to the squeaks as he chewed. A few of the dairies in the UP still carried 'squeaky cheese', and Roy knew them all.

They continued on to the Soo and had lunch at the Freighters Restaurant in the Ojibway Hotel. Roy liked the Freighters because it was so close to the Locks and the Sunday Brunch was one of his favorites. From the dining room they watched the Ziemie Suwalska, a 591 foot Polish 'salty', slowly approaching the Soo Locks from the East.

Later they climbed the observation stand to look down on the 850 foot Roger Blough as it entered the Poe Lock from the West. The Poe Lock, named after a civil engineer, is the only lock in the entire St. Lawrence system wide enough for gigantic 1,000 foot long, 105 foot wide self-unloading lake freighters. The Roger Blough is the only 850 footer with a 105 foot beam. All 'salties' are small enough to go through any lock in the St. Lawrence system, so the Ziemie Suwalska was aimed at the MacArthur Lock. The captains of the lake freighters were licensed to take their ships through the Soo Locks, but all 'Salties' had to be guided through the locks by a licensed U.S. steersman.

After watching the two ships trade sea levels, Roy gave Luana an abbreviated tour of the rest of the town, including the campus of Lake Superior State University. Then they headed South toward Pickford and down to Hessel and Cedarville to see the Les Cheneaux Islands. It was after eight o'clock by the time they reached the Mackinac Bridge and Mackinaw Village and they were both exhausted. Roy had enjoyed his tour guide status so much he was already planning the next trip.

"Let's see, tomorrow we'll take the ferry to Mackinac Island; we'll rent bicycles and ride around the Island. It's eight miles and it's great exercise, and you'll finally see the Grand Hotel and the Belgians and the Clydesdales and..."

Luana interrupted with a smile, "and... and, just wait one minute, Professor Nelson. I'm so tired I couldn't even think about anything but that nice quiet, comfortable, couch on the porch. Wait till I wake up tomorrow, then you can tell me about it."

She dozed off on the couch shortly after watching the blazing sun drop off the edge of Lake Michigan. Roy woke her up and helped her to her bedroom after the eleven o'clock news.

Luana talked Roy into spending Monday relaxing by the water, "let's go to the Island on Tuesday or Wednesday; I know I'll enjoy it more by then." Roy curtailed his anticipation and politely acquiesced.

On Tuesday morning, Clayton was returning from his two-day shift on the Coast Guard Cutter, Mackinaw, which was stationed in Cheboygan. The Mackinaw, at 290 feet, is the largest ice breaker in the U.S. Great Lakes fleet. Clayton spent a two or three-day shift on board ship patrolling the Straits and Lake Huron waters.

He was in the habit of walking next door to say hello to Roy. Now, it would be an excuse to see Luana again. He knocked on Roy's roadside porch door. There was no answer. The car was in the driveway. Clayton walked around the cottage to the waterside porch and saw a neatly cut square hole in the glass above the door handle. He thrust open the door and found Luana tied up and gagged, lying on the bed in the guest bedroom. He untied her and pulled off the gag. Clayton searched the other rooms in the small cottage, but Roy was conspicuously absent. It took Luana a few minutes to get her blood circulating freely in her hands and feet. Clayton helped her walk around the room, then let her rest again.

"There now, Luana, can you tell me what happened?"

Luana didn't have much to describe, "We both went to bed after the 11:00 news. Sometime in the middle of the night there was a clinking sound, and within seconds a man grabbed me around the neck, pressed something into my face and I passed out. I didn't really see anyone or anything. I could see the clock when I woke up, it was 9 something in the morning. Where is Ro..., where is Professor Nelson?"

"I'm afraid he's missing, and we have no idea where. But I think we both know why."

Luana tried not to show the emotional impact Roy's

disappearance had on her in front of Clayton, she just said, "we must find him."

14

THE Fujima is a bulk carrier, diesel driven, ocean freighter registered in Japan. It is 575 feet in length and 75 feet at the beam. It had traveled from Tokyo to Honolulu, through the Panama Canal, up to the St. Lawrence River, past Montreal, and through a series of locks lifting it 226 feet to Lake Ontario. It then passed through the Welland Canal, a series of seven lift locks and one guard lock, at 1380 feet, the longest, but not the largest, lock in the world, lifting the Fujima another 326 feet, from Lake Ontario to Lake Erie. It traveled past Detroit and Lake St. Clair into

Lake Huron and was heading for the Straits of Mackinac.

At about 30 minutes from the bridge the Fujima checked in with the Coast Guard. Clayton happened to be chatting with the radio operator on the Coast Guard cutter, Mackinaw, and he heard, but paid little attention, as his buddy recorded the Fujima's location, direction, and the time of the communication. Ships were not officially required to check in after their first port of entry, but because of the numerous ferries that had to cross the freighter channel in the Straits, the Coast Guard requested that all lakers and 'salties' give the 30 minute warning.

The Fujima's destination was Chicago, where it would discharge its cargo, mainly retail store merchandise. The next day it would head up Lake Michigan, past the bridge, in front of the Grand Hotel, up the St. Mary's River to the Soo Locks, using the MacArthur or the Poe Lock. The sign at the model of the Poe Lock in the visitor's park states that it is larger than any other lock in the Great Lakes, the St. Lawrence Seaway, the Panama Canal, Europe and Asia. Roy and Eleanor always wondered why it seemed to 'beat around the bush'. One day they asked a security guard if the sign meant that it was the largest lock in the world, but he didn't know either.

The Fujima would sometimes travel the length of Lake Superior, the largest and deepest fresh water lake in the world, to Duluth, Minnesota, load a cargo of wheat and head back for Japan. But this time the Fujima was going only as far as Algoma Steel Company at Sault Ste. Marie, Canada for a load of specialized steel for a member of the Japanese Global Trade Organization.

Roy was now part of the cargo of the Fujima, heading for Chicago, courtesy of the impeccable planning of

Amos and Andy. The Fujima had passed directly under the bridge at 4:10 a.m. on Tuesday morning. Roy's cottage was one and one-half miles west of the bridge. The channel that all Westbound ships followed was about two miles from Roy's shoreline. The Fujima, coming from the South, East of the bridge, would have to follow the channel between the green and red buoys, which directed them to the center of the bridge, and then Westward to Lake Michigan.

A motorized rubber dinghy could be launched from the outside of the Fujima when it reached the wide channel between Round Island and Mackinaw Village. It would be able to cut across closer to the shoreline, undetected, considering the time of year and the time of night, and travel at least three miles shorter than the Fujima's route. Amos and Andy figured that the Fujima was traveling at a speed that would allow them thirty minutes to get to Roy's cottage and back to the ship in their dinghy.

They reached the shoreline of the wooded section to the North of the cottage. They skillfully cut the glass in the door above the handle, opened the door quietly and stealthily followed their flawless pattern of operation. Amos went quickly to Roy's room, gripped him in a headlock and chloroformed him in a matter of seconds. Andy moved to Luana's room, put his left arm around her neck and squeezed until she was almost unconscious, chloroformed her and then proceeded to gag and tie her hands and feet.

The two men were heavily muscled and about the average height of most Japanese men. The dinghy easily made it back to the Fujima as it rounded the Straits into Lake Michigan. Roy, with hands and feet tied, was placed in a small room in the cargo hold. When he woke up he tried to figure out an explanation for this turn of events. He was certain that someone wanted to interrogate him or he would have been tossed into Lake Michigan by this time.

The Fujima was docked and unloading its cargo at Chicago on Wednesday morning. Captain Taro Ozeki was in his spacious cabin speaking in English with Mitsuo Fuchida and Saburo Shindo. Robert's Information Network Center referred to them as 'Amos' and 'Andy'.

Captain Ozeki had been able to join the Japanese Navy in 1944, when he was seventeen. The Japanese Navy had already endured humiliating defeats at the hands of the American Navy and, along with his countrymen, Captain Ozeki suffered the indignity of the Japanese surrender in 1945.

He was never able to uncouple himself from the humiliation. He became the leader of a small group of vindictive, jingoistic, Japanese nationals who cooperated with the growing organized crime system, the Japanese 'yakuza'. One of the large 'yakuza' crime families was placing its major emphasis on controlling the U.S. auto parts industry. Captain Ozeki was a key instrument in the overall strategy.

Mitsuo Fuchida and Saburo Shindo were both named after their famous uncles who led the first and second waves of the air attacks on Pearl Harbor. As young men, because of their heritage, they were repeatedly invited to meetings of the anti-American 'jingoist' radicals who treated them as heroes. At each meeting the members ceremoniously revived the memory of the infamous attack on December 7, 1941. The Japanese planes, led by Captain Fuchida and Lt. Shindo, destroyed 165 American aircraft, sunk or severely damaged eighteen battleships, cruisers, destroyers and other U.S. Navy ships, and killed approximately 2,400

Americans, soldiers and civilians. In ten minutes, they left 1,170 unsuspecting sailors trapped in the hull of the battleship, Arizona, to reside forever in a watery grave. They lost only 29 planes in the two-hour attack.

Thrown together frequently at the meetings, Fuchida and Shindo eventually became inseparable friends and both became committed to the cause. They joined Captain Ozeki's group, which had the same philosophy and craving for revenge. They spent their young lives training for violence. In Tokyo they both worked at a travel agency owned by the group so their frequent absences would go unnoticed. They both attended English classes in Tokyo throughout their teens and spent a year at UCLA to learn the American customs. They and Captain Ozeki had learned to speak English devoid of the customary oriental inflections.

"She wants him alive." the Captain said.

"She must find out exactly how much he knows and if anyone else knows anything, like that Hawaiian girl."

"That's crazy, we should get rid of him now," offered Fuchida.

"It's too risky, this ship is too important. If there was a slip and the body was traced to the Fujima... it's not worth the risk," the Captain insisted.

"We will proceed as planned. After we finish here, we'll leave in time to allow us to reach the Straits about midnight. The Straits are always calm at midnight. When we've just passed between the two lighthouses and the Mackinac Island harbor you will take Nelson in the dinghy to Mission Point. I will instruct Fraulein Schwartz to have Wilhelm, she calls him William, help you get him to the house."

After thinking for a minute the Captain added, "the schedule I gave to the U.S. Customs reports us directly under the bridge at 1:00 a.m. All foreign ships must report their itinerary and other information to U.S. Customs at the first point of entry, which is at the Snell Lock in the St. Lawrence. In addition, all ships give a courtesy warning to the Coast Guard at thirty minutes before passing the Mackinac Bridge.

We'll reach the bridge an hour earlier than my official itinerary shows when I report in to the Cheboygan Coast Guard, which also has access to my itinerary. So I'll just explain that we got an early start. That'll give us a better chance that the area will be free of any nosy ships. No one must see the dinghy leaving the Fujima or there would be an inquiry. You'll launch on the Round Island side, which has few inhabitants... but, let's wait until we get there and I'll give you instructions."

Amos and Andy were in no position to argue with the Captain about the plan. They were accustomed to following his orders, and they knew that the Captain was meticulous in planning every move. His ship moved freely back and forth between Japan and the United States serving Takeda's 'yakuza'-owned businesses in the Japanese Global Trade Organization. He also offered his services to other Japanese business groups that would undermine the fair trade and friendly relations between the United States and Japan. Captain Ozeki had an uneasy feeling about this trip. It involved a risk of detection far greater than that of the Fujima's more routine missions. But he had his orders, and they must be followed.

Captain Ozeki had great respect for Fuchida and Shindo, but he had the last word and considered the matter closed. Later that day he noted an article on the business page of the Chicago Tribune. The article described how Michigan's Governor Hansler was to meet tomorrow with Japanese Minister of Trade, Tomizo

Eda, and several European trade ministers to discuss the international problems in the auto parts industry.

15

IT was Wednesday, July 15. In Lansing, Governor Hansler's meeting was to begin in one hour. He was speaking on his unlisted personal phone line with Ito Takeda.

"I'm sorry, Mr. Takeda, you are not invited to this meeting. It is exclusively for official trade ministers; in fact, only two representatives of the state legislature are invited, and even the press has been excluded at Mr. Eda's request."

"Governor Hansler, you know you can persuade Eda to put my name on the list. I should be there to defend the position of my trade organization. I don't mean to bring it up, but... you know what I mean. You had better try harder to convince him," Takeda threatened.

"It's too late to get you in now, but I will protect your interests, don't you worry. But, don't call me again on this line. Who gave you this number?"

The question was rhetorical, the Governor knew very well who gave Takeda his number. Governor Hansler had invited one Republican, his close associate, State Senator Larry Trump and one Democrat, State Senator Pam Lehto, a Finnish-American from Iron River in the Upper Peninsula, to the meeting. The European trade ministers were from Britain, France, Germany, Italy and Holland. The Governor closed the meeting to the press, giving security as the reason, but actually Mr. Eda had insisted on it.

The British minister admonished, "In order to stop this price fixing, and U.S. income tax avoidance practiced by our Japanese friends, your government will have to establish uniform and fair rules of operation. Right now the Japanese companies find legal loopholes faster than you Yanks get around to plugging them up."

The other European ministers agreed.

"It is unfair to the rest of us," added the German trade minister, "we play the competitive game fairly, actually in accordance with American guidelines. The Japanese assemblers are forcing our parts suppliers out of business along with the American parts people."

Governor Hansler was about to speak up for Mr. Eda, who was accustomed to Japan bashing, but the Japanese trade minister was determined to confess some internal problems not previously disclosed.

Mr. Eda began, "the Japanese parent companies of the six auto assembly plants that are operating in "Auto Alley" and the one in California are now following the U.S. laws as well as their unwritten competitive practices to the letter. I admit, they were taking every competitive advantage and tax loophole possible up to January 1 of this year. Now, we are faced with a serious internal problem that will affect the honest Japanese auto parts producers as well as your companies."

The room was silent; it was certainly not customary for a Japanese official of this stature to admit an internal weakness.

Mr. Eda continued, "Organized crime has mushroomed recently in Japan, centered in Tokyo. It is called the 'yakuza'. They now control entire industries. Their tactics are ruthless and they are giving enormous bribes to the police. You Americans must remember that after the war you helped us to develop a peaceful society; one which did not depend on military or police force. Forty years later we find that we are inexperienced in crime control. We are living in the 1990's with law enforcement systems of the 1950's."

Eda continued, "a trade group called the Japanese Global Trade Organization, using the acronym, JGTO, is a front for investing 'yakuza' crime profits. About one-half of the members of this group are legitimate businesses and the other half are owned by 'yakuza' families, under pyramids of assumed names. No one is supposed to know which are legitimate, and which are not, except their representative, Mr. Ito Takeda. The JGTO now controls over 50% of the auto parts production in Japan. Over 40% of their production is exported to the U.S. and another 20% to Europe."

Tomizo Eda excused himself for a minute, walked over to Governor Hansler and they whispered to each other for a few seconds. The Governor announced,

"Mr. Eda asks that what he reveals to you be kept strictly confidential. Would you be so kind as to give him your word. As you know, your word is as good as a written contract in the Japanese culture."

Each minister and senator, individually assured Mr. Eda that he or she would not reveal the events of the meeting. Mr. Eda accepted their word, assuming, perhaps naively, that personal integrity and honor were as important to them as it was to him.

Mr. Eda began, speaking in a low voice as if to denote the secrecy of his message, "I have in my possession a list of all of the auto parts manufacturers and assemblers operating in the U.S. that are owned by my country's organized crime group, the 'yakuza'. I cannot reveal the source of the information, because I have given my word. Strangely enough it is not Japanese.

The source is a cooperative, and highly secretive, global organization that provides information to any government that seriously makes an effort to counteract international crime. We have been promised a list of the 'yakuza'-owned companies operating in Europe at a later date, and I have been told that this list will take several more weeks to compile. When it is ready, I will personally deliver a copy to each trade minister present here today. It is required that I must deliver these lists myself."

The Japanese minister continued, "I will give the list with the 'yakuza' controlled firms located in the United States to Governor Hansler. Governor, you must come to my hotel room at noon tomorrow. I will personally hand it only to you; no one else may come in your place. I am in suite 801 at the Capital City Hotel. You may use whatever methods you wish with the list of firms, but I suggest that your government neutralize them somehow."

Mr. Eda chuckled, "You Europeans may wish to follow the American method; announce that you suspect a toxic waste deposit under their plant. The environmental activists will picket for months. Send the police in to arrest them, which will interfere with their operations. That will give you time to hassle them with lawsuits and fines."

"It is imperative that we stop them," Mr. Eda emphasized. "Our countries must support a free trade policy that is fair to all of us. The Japanese are learning this the hard way, because nations are closing their doors to our goods. Now that we are finally pursuing the policies that I have been advocating, this ugly monster rears its head, and it must be stopped. Will you help me?"

The ministers and senators were overwhelmed by the sincerity and spirit of Mr. Eda. They all assured him of their support and secrecy. It was not difficult to understand why secrecy was necessary. The 'yakuza' would not hesitate to stop his crusade.

16

ACK in Mackinaw Village, Clayton and Luana reviewed every detail. They scoured the cottage for notes, just in case Roy had recorded something he hadn't told them about. Clayton found evidence in front of the cottage that a small boat had been pulled up on shore.

"What did Roy say that ship was named?" Clayton had never actually heard Roy say the name, but remembered that Robert had told Roy about a Japanese ship.

Luana remembered the name, "it was the Fujima."

Clayton almost shouted, "How dumb can I get! The Fujima, I heard it check in at the Straits Tuesday morning. That's it! That's it! Roy was taken to the Fujima."

Luana was so elated that she threw her arms around Clayton and gave him a kiss on the cheek. Clayton's heart skipped a beat. He spontaneously grabbed her tight in his powerful arms and gave her a real kiss, a long kiss. Luana was stunned with mixed feelings; she could have resisted more, but she didn't.

Clayton, taking Roy's admonitions seriously, was embarrassed and apologetic, "I'm sorry, Luana... I got carried away for a minute. I don't have to tell you how... well... just how damn pretty you are, and I don't have the self control that Roy has."

"Oh, I understand Clayton; we were both excited."

Clayton knew her elation would end as soon as she realized why Roy was taken to the Fujima. It could be for only one reason, to eliminate him, just as they did Professor Makinen and Harold Martin.

Could Roy be still alive? Luana tried not to think negatively about it. She knew that Roy could be at the bottom of Lake Michigan. Yet, like Roy with Eleanor, she would never accept it.

Clayton checked with the Coast Guard Station and wrote down the schedule of the Fujima. It would reach the Straits at 1:00 a.m. on Thursday morning. Clayton and Luana decided that they would be on Clayton's 35 foot Chris Craft to meet the Fujima, and to rescue Roy, assuming that he is still alive.

During their search for an explanation of Roy's disappearance. Luana had called Martha, thinking that she might have some helpful information. She was completely unaware of Martha's feelings for Roy. So she was surprised when Martha said she would grab everything, pertaining to Roy's inquiries, and drive straight to Mackinaw Village. She arrived at seven p.m. on Tuesday evening. Clayton went to Cheboygan for supplies while the two ladies went to Audie's Restaurant for dinner. Neither Luana nor Martha had stopped to eat with all the excitement.

When Martha met Luana she was stunned. Martha had fallen head over heels in love with the grown up, sophisticated, scholarly, dignified and, in her eyes, handsome, Roy she had only known as a boy. After Luana called, she dashed to Mackinaw out of her desperation to help him. Her spinning, emotionally confused mind didn't pause to wonder who Luana was.

Luana was cold water splashed in her face. Martha had become an attractive 48 year old woman, but she was no match for this 38 year old former beauty queen. She had been unrealistic to think that she could just jump into Roy's life and say, "here I am, please fall in love with me." She couldn't imagine that even Roy could resist this young, entrancing, Polynesian beauty sleeping in the same cottage.

The two ladies were cautiously polite to each other as they devoured a fillet of broiled whitefish with morel sauce, a specialty of Audie's gourmet chef. Martha broke the spell by bluntly asking, "are you in love with Roy?"

Luana hesitated before answering, as if she were in a televised political debate, "I admire him. He and Eleanor were good friends of my Mother. I guess I have a deep concern for him."

Martha teased, "you didn't answer my question."

Luana displayed a little more emotion, "It's because I can't. Roy may be dead. And if he's alive, he is still in love with Eleanor. He won't accept her death as long as there is no absolute proof. Whether he's alive or not, only a fool would want to be in love with him."

There was a moment of silence while the two ladies digested their food as well as that last statement. Luana liked Martha's honest frankness and Martha couldn't help but like Luana's genuine sweetness.

"Martha, I know that Roy would want you to know everything now. He's in great danger; he probably told you he was writing a book, but it is far more than that. Professor Makinen and Harold Martin were both killed to keep them from exposing a secret about the Governor. And although I don't exactly understand all the implications, the Japanese underworld is involved, and they're going to kill Roy, unless we can stop them. Do you want to help Clayton and me? We plan on trying to save him, if... if he is still alive."

"Thank you, Luana, Roy and I grew up together, like a brother and sister," she added gratuitously. "I wouldn't think of turning down a chance to help him."

Clayton trained the girls in the operation of the Nicolet all day Wednesday. He wanted them to be able to take over from him if he were detained, or in case of any emergency situation.

The Fujima was still docked at Chicago. Captain Ozeki received a phone call in his quarters. After the call he went directly to the cabin of Amos and Andy. The two men were playing cards. There was money on the table. After a few minutes and a short conversion with the two men Captain Ozeki left their cabin.

An hour later the Fujima began its trip North through Lake Michigan toward the Straits of Mackinac. Back in the cabin of Amos and Andy, there was no more card game. Amos was all alone in the cabin, smoking a huge Havana cigar, and reading a Tokyo newspaper.

The Fujima checked in with the Coast Guard at a position Southwest of the bridge at 11:30 p.m. Captain

Ozeki explained that he left Chicago an hour earlier than planned, and that he would be passing the bridge in 30 minutes. The Officer on duty recorded the change in time and seemed to be unconcerned about the reason. "I'll report your estimated time of arrival to the Soo Locks, they will put you through the Poe Lock, since they are still dredging the MacArthur", he courteously informed Captain Ozeki.

Clayton was in Roy's cottage with Luana and Martha. He had the scanner turned on and heard the conversation between the Coast Guard and Captain Ozeki. He had planned on leaving at midnight so that he would at Mackinac Island at 12:30 a.m. That would give them one-half hour to prepare for the arrival of the Fujima. Now the Fujima would be at the bridge at midnight and in front of the Grand Hotel and the Mackinac Island Harbor ten minutes later.

About 9:00 p.m. he had told the ladies to get some sleep. They lay down, already dressed for the journey, but found it impossible to sleep. When Clayton yelled they were up and ready; they all piled in the powerful Chris Craft and took off for the Island.

Clayton explained his plan as they started out, "You see, we'll go along the shoreline and then between piers 15 and 16. After that we'll head straight for the Island. This way the Fujima won't be able to spot us. There aren't many pleasure boats out at this time of night, so we might be conspicuous."

Martha had been to Mackinaw Village and to Mackinac Island a few times, but she had never seen this awesome panoramic view from Roy's cottage area before. The night was cool and the sky was perfectly clear. The enormous bridge was lighted from end to end. The cables were covered with bright red, white, blue and yellow lights; the water was perfectly still causing the reflection of the lights to stretch almost to the shore. The Grand Hotel was like a sparkling diamond bracelet. Awesome was the only generation gap word she could think of to describe the scene.

Clayton continued, "I figure it this way. If Roy is dead, and we all hope that isn't the case, we have nothing to lose. We are just out for a midnight joy ride. However, if Roy is still alive, that female Nazi at the Governor's Mansion wants to question him and then kill him or have one those mafia boys do it for her.

The reason that they didn't drop him off at Mackinac Island on the way going to Chicago was that the Fujima doesn't pass close enough to the Island. On the return trip from Chicago to the Soo Locks, all ships must go between the narrow passage in front of the Island. The shipping lane is within a few hundred feet of the shore. At night they can launch a dinghy and get to shore without being seen."

He switched to an instructive posture in his voice, "you see, a foreign ship may not send any small boats ashore. Some two hundred or more foreign registered ships go through the St. Lawrence each season, from March to December. Think of all the illegal aliens and drugs that could be sent ashore. So the narrow passage between Mackinac Island on one side and the almost uninhabited Round Island on the other side, during the darkness of night, gives them the perfect opportunity to take Roy ashore."

"Now this is our revised plan, since we have a late start. We should be at the Marina at about," looking at his watch, "12:15, and they will pass at... oh my.... damn! they will get there five minutes before us. I planned on an extra half hour. Let me think."

Clayton was reaching for a solution, "Ok, I've got it. They won't launch a dinghy if they see us, so we'll start out from the back side of Round Island so I can stay just out of sight. When they pass the lighthouses, we'll come in slowly from behind them. You girls will have to help me. One of you go up front and guide me in as soon as you see the stern..., that is, the back of the Fujima. But, you must keep it just barely in sight and watch for the dinghy. Once they launch it we can follow it in."

Martha's bright mind wanted to know, "if they see us coming won't they just toss Roy overboard? His hands will be tied and won't he.....drown?" Luana grimaced, but kept quiet.

Clayton agreed, "Ok, we'll hold back. If we let them reach shore, it will be safer for Roy. We know where they will take him, so we can intercept them by taking a shortcut up to Turkey Hill Road above Market Street. How does that sound?"

Although they didn't have any idea about the directions, Martha and Luana were relieved; both had visualized Roy, with his hands tied, sinking to the bottom of the channel. If Clayton's assumptions are correct, the purpose of this entire effort is to take Roy to Hilda alive, not dead. Any interference before Roy is taken ashore would be too risky.

The Fujima passed the bridge and the Grand Hotel as Clayton and his crew eased along the shoreline of Round Island. Martha was up front. "Nothing yet," she shouted back. The Fujima passed the harbor slowly.

"They should launch now," Clayton insisted.

"No, not yet. They seem to be rounding a curve. There is a large building on the left. There... there goes something small in back of the Fujima and heading toward that building," Martha reported much like a newswoman on prime time.

"You mean they didn't get off at the docks?" Clayton questioned, not expecting an answer.

Clayton didn't expect them to go in at the convention center of the Mission Point Resort. The building had been the library of the Moral Rearmament Movement's College founded by Rex Humbard in the 60's. After several changes in ownership the old college dormitories were converted to hotel rooms and the other buildings remodeled into a first class vacation resort.

He immediately wheeled his Chris Craft into the Mackinac Island Marina, without any communication with the Island. He pulled into an empty slip close to shore, cut the motor and tied up as quickly as possible. Martha and Luana acted like old deck hands, helping Clayton and running after him down the dock to shore, Luana with a paddle in her hand.

Clayton led them through Marquette Park to Fort Street and then left on Turkey Hill Road. Turkey Hill Road was the road below the Governor's Mansion. Instead of walking around on the road Clayton led them straight up the steep hill to the top. Clayton then selected a secluded spot slightly above the Governor's Mansion, where they could watch the house and the road in both directions. Clayton knew that there were two circuitous carriage routes from the docks to the Mansion; the most logical approach would be the shorter one from the East.

17

C APTAIN Ozeki personally helped Amos pull a drugged Roy into a small, rubber dinghy. He didn't want his crew to know any more than they had to about his clandestine operations. The dinghy was launched on the Round Island side of the ship. Amos had to row the dinghy away from the side of the Fujima while it passed by. He then rowed straight for shore on the grounds of the Mission Point Resort. William was there to meet Amos. He was driving a small dray pulled by Bessie and Al, the slow, but reliable, Clydesdales. All transporting on the Island is done by horse-driven flat carts, or drays, the larger ones pulled by two-horse teams.

William and Amos loaded Roy unto the dray and covered him with the light rubber dinghy. Bessie and Al trudged up steep Truscott Street to Huron Road, the long sloping road that passed in front of Fort Mackinac, and ended in front of the Governor's Mansion. Huron Road then connected with Annex Road that meandered around to the horse barns and eventually led to the side of the Grand Hotel. It was a slow, circular trek, the Clydesdale team being rested occasionally on the way up the steep hill.

Roy woke up from his stupor as the dray reached the top of the hill. It took a while to reconstruct the turn of events. His head was throbbing from the effects of the drug. His hands were tied, but his feet were free. The rubber dinghy over him was light and he was able to move enough to see where they were. He recognized the fort entrance as they passed and knew that the Governor's Mansion was just a hundred yards or so down the road. Wilhelm was asking Amos if he planned on reboarding the Fujima.

"I don't know," Amos said. "I just follow orders."

Amos knew perfectly well what his plans were, but he and Andy never revealed their orders nor discussed their itinerary with anyone. Their orders came from only one source in the 'yakuza'. But the 'yakuza' had become complex, with competing families no longer working for the same purposes. Amos and Andy had learned to trust no one except their mentor, Captain Ozeki. They suspected, but were never directly told, that Captain Ozeki reported to Ito Takeda, Director of the Japanese Global Trade Organization.

Wilhelm had no use for the 'Japs' and his tight-mouthed ally irritated him.

"If you 'Japs' had finished the job at Pearl Harbor we would have won the war," he badgered. You should have invaded the Islands and sunk every ship in the fleet. Instead, your dumb forefathers let the Yanks rebuild the whole fleet, except the Arizona and a couple others. If they had taken Hawaii, you 'Japs' could have ruled the Pacific."

Amos was furious with his abrasive Nazi companion, but was trained to perfection in reacting objectively to verbal abuse.

"If you studied an unbiased version of history, my friend, you would know that Hitler's foolish attempt to invade Russia is what lost the war. He became an absolute madman and destroyed the German war machine."

As the two were embroiled in their verbal discord, Roy quietly slipped off the back end of the dray. He hit the ground with his buttocks to absorb the short fall. He had waited for the perfect moment when the two were in the middle of their conversation and when the road turned just enough so he could quickly roll off to the side out of sight. He ran silently into the woods above the Fort and disappeared. He had been working on the ropes around his hands since he woke up.

He came upon Custer Road near Skull Cave. He knew he was close to the Mackinac Island cemeteries. He remembered a metal fence around the graves of British soldiers killed in the battles for the Island in the Revolutionary War and the War of 1812. Or was the fence around the graves of the French soldiers? Whatever! He found what was left of the old, rusted, broken metal fence and easily cut through the ropes. Roy's muscles were cramped and aching from almost three days of inactivity.

He hobbled for a while until he loosened up. He took

a circular path that he instinctively knew would lead him to the grounds of the Grand Hotel. He followed Carriage Road, which would take him to West Bluff Road, so that he could come in to the Grand Hotel grounds from the West end. They would never expect him to follow such a roundabout path.

When Clayton saw the dray coming up the road from the direction of the Fort, he led his companions to the thick bushes along the path leading to the Governor's Mansion. The dray pulled in front of the Governor's Mansion and both men hopped off to unload their human cargo. Clayton tried to persuade his two companions to stay out of the action, but they insisted on backing him up. Luana had her paddle ready and Martha grabbed a small tree branch.

"He's gone," yelled Wilhelm, as he lifted the rubber dinghy up off the dray. Amos, sizing up the situation without exclamation, ran back over the road they had travelled, darting in and out of the woods as he searched for Roy. Wilhelm followed after Amos, both men cursing each other in their native languages.

Clayton realized what had happened when he saw the two men scurrying around and yelling at each other. He turned and with Luana and Martha following, crouched unnoticed through the bushes to the steep hillside on the other side of the house. They proceeded to climb cautiously down to Turkey Hill Road on the next lower level.

"Where would Roy go? Martha wondered out loud. Clayton guessed that he would head toward the Marina. Roy didn't know that they were there to rescue him, and there is no Coast Guard Station or State Police Post on the Island, just the local police, who ride bicycles. So he would hope to find someone awake on one of the pleasure boats docked overnight at the

Marina. Having no better prediction the two tired ladies followed Clayton down the road to the lower level of the fort, which led directly to the Marina.

In the excitement of the events, both Luana and Martha realized that Roy was alive. Now, when the tense moments awaiting their unpredictable encounter with the kidnappers were over, they both felt the emotional impact of his return from the dead. That is, as Martha had put it earlier, the likelihood of Roy's being dead was greater than that of his being alive. And Luana, although she would never admit it, was deeply pessimistic when she assembled all of the facts in her mind. Now, Luana was exhilarated by the knowledge that Roy was alive somewhere out there in the woods.

"Clayton, we've got to find Roy... Professor Nelson... before those terrible men... what can we do?" Luana queried. Martha was too exhausted to even speak from the running and climbing. But for Luana, who swam in the ocean almost every day since she was a child, this was no more than a little exercise.

"We'll go directly to the Nicolet and wait," Clayton insisted. When they arrived at the docks, Clayton jumped into the Nicolet and prepared everything for a quick takeoff. Martha was with him and Luana stood on shore looking down the walkway.

After telling Martha how to start the motor, Clayton walked over to Luana so he wouldn't have to shout.

"Go down to the Chippewa Hotel, Luana. From there you can see anyone coming along Huron Street. I'll watch in the other direction. He doesn't know we're here so he'll try to avoid being seen. We've got to see him first, so hide behind something. And we don't want to be seen by those crums either."

Roy came out of the woods at West Bluff Road, which ran directly in front of the Grand Hotel. Instead of going down the road he entered the front porch from the West side and, acting like a typical guest, walked nonchalantly down the main entrance stairway to the pool at the lower level. The only difference was that it was about 1 or 2 in the morning, and not many guests were heading for the pool at that time. Roy knew that there was a path from the pool area to Lakeshore Boulevard, the road which circled the Island along the water. He was able to reach Lakeshore Boulevard in a matter of minutes and proceeded along the boardwalk, which became the West end of Huron Street, the main tourist street.

Amos and Wilhelm were not anxious to face Hilda. They had been searching aimlessly for Roy until they finally realized that they were wasting time.

Wilhelm said, "he'll head for the docks, he won't want to stay on the Island very long." No argument from Amos, which meant that they would rather look for Roy once more before they faced the fury of Wilhelm's boss.

Luana saw a figure sneaking along the storefronts coming along Huron Street toward the Marina. As he approached Luana stood in plain sight in front of the Chippewa so Roy would see her and not panic.

She constrained her emotions as she hugged him saying, "Prof... Roy, I'm so thankful you're alive. We were afraid you were dead."

Their embrace was platonic, even though Luana's feelings were compelling. But, this was no time to let affection interfere with the urgency of the moment.

Roy, seeing Clayton at the other end of the Marina, was elated by the unexpected rescue. He grabbed Luana's hand and they raced toward the Nicolet. Clayton saw them and also headed for the Nicolet. They all jumped aboard, Martha started the engine, and Clayton freed the ropes from the dock before he jumped in and took over the helm.

As the Nicolet was maneuvering out of the Marina slip, Amos and Wilhelm came running across Marquette Park in front of the Marina. Wilhelm had a pistol, but he wouldn't dare fire it on Mackinac Island, where, with no noisy automobiles and a family tourist trade, a pistol shot in the middle of the night would wake up the whole Island.

The Nicolet escaped into the Straits and headed for Mackinaw Village. It was Martha's turn to give Roy a big hug. By this time Roy was beginning to feel the great sensation of being free again. He talked all the way back. At the center of the Mackinac Bridge, they passed to the port side of the Edwin H. Gott, a magnificent 1,004 foot US Steel-owned laker. It was lighted from bow to stern. To the lone truckdriver, passing over the Bridge, the Nicolet must have looked like a mouse beside an elephant.

When Roy stopped talking for a minute, they started singing. Luana was the only one who could sing in tune, but they were all too happy to worry about that. They all slept at Clayton's cottage that night. But before Clayton would retire he called Paul Tamber, who was in the squad car that night, and asked him to keep an eye on his and Roy's cottage for the next few days.

Amos and Wilhelm returned to the Governor's Mansion grumbling all the way. Hilda had seen the commotion after Roy escaped and waited impatiently, wondering where her subordinates were. She was furious with both of them when they tried to explain. They had blundered, but they were too arrogant to admit it. So each tried to blame it on the other; animosity between them had reached an explosive level.

Hilda, sensing a problem, said, "what's done is done. Now we know that the Professor has three friends who probably know too much. They must be silenced, but, it's late now. Get some sleep and I'll decide what to do tomorrow."

By the next morning, however, Amos was gone; he was on the eight o'clock ferry for St. Ignace. He had the $1.89 breakfast special at the local Big Boy, which included two eggs, bacon and sausage, and two pieces of cheese toast. Amos had acquired an appreciation for American style breakfasts when he lived in California. After breakfast he rented a car and drove to Hessel and Cedarville, and turned North to Pickford, where they pastured the Clydedales, Percherons and Belgians from Mackinac Island in the Winter. He then turned East toward Barbeau. After driving about ten miles he came to a stop sign. On one corner was the Barbeau Post Office. There were no buildings on the other three corners. There were no stores, no gas stations, not one building in sight anywhere. He drove on about three miles, where the road ended at the water. There were cottages along the banks of the narrow water passage, but still no sign of a town. On the other side of the 200 foot wide channel was Neebish Island, home to about 25 year round residents.

All ships travelling downbound from the Soo Locks to Lake Huron must pass through the thirty-five mile narrow channel between the U.S. and Canada that connects Lake Superior and Lake Huron. There is only about a twenty-three foot difference in the levels of the two Great Lakes. The St. Mary's Rapids, about one-quarter of a mile wide and three-quarters of a mile in length, are bypassed by the locks. The channel is so narrow at Neebish Island that upbound ships have to be routed to the North side of the Island and downbound ships to the South. The South channel, being too shallow, had been dredged out to accommodate the 1,000 footers and the 'Salties', the local marine term for the foreign freighters.

A 'salty' had just gone through the Soo locks and would reach the downbound side of Neebish Island in about thirty minutes, at about 1:30 p.m., Thursday afternoon. The white painted name on the bow of the ocean-worn freighter was 'Fujima'.

Amos arrived at the ferry dock to Neebish Island a few minutes after 12:00 noon. Although there were no stores, just a few small houses near the dock, Amos wondered if this might be Barbeau. He had not passed anything else that looked like a town, even though he was following the signs along the way pointing to Barbeau. The small ferry had just left at noon and the next would leave at 2:00 p.m. There was, of course, no rental car office at the ferry dock. So Amos had paid extra for the pickup of the car by the St. Ignace Office. He parked and locked the rental car near the ferry dock, as prearranged, and walked along the shoreline until he located a secluded spot. Here he could easily swim to the center of the channel where all freighters must travel. In fact, the channel was so narrow at this point that the 1,000 footers were only about 50 feet from shoreline.

These were the directions that Captain Ozeki had given him; a rope ladder would be waiting for him at the side of the ship. The exact spot, which minimized detection, had been selected by the circumspect Captain. Amos was amazed as he watched a light fog drift into the channel from the direction of Lake Huron at about fifteen minutes before the Fujima was expected.

"Did the omniscient Captain Ozeki arrange for this too?" He chuckled to himself.

18

CLAYTON bought a Detroit newspaper at the grocery store on Friday morning. One of the main stories was "Japanese Trade Minister Falls to Death from Lansing hotel room." The story described that Mr. Tomizo Eda, Minister of Trade from Japan, had fallen from the eighth story window of his room in the Capital City Hotel in downtown Lansing. He was in Lansing attending an important series of meetings with U.S. legislators and business representatives. The police would not comment on the possibility of foul play, even though it was hinted that Mr. Eda may have been pushed. However, any admission of murder would increase the possibility of international complications.

Clayton scouted around and found a Lansing paper. Someone leaked information to a nosy reporter that the Governor had an appointment with Mr. Eda on Thursday at noon. The source claimed that the Governor's appointment calendar for Thursday showed that he had an appointment for noon that was crossed out. The Governor's Office flatly denied any such arrangement, but confirmed that Mr. Eda had met with the Governor, two state senators and several European trade ministers on Wednesday. Eda died at exactly 10:25 on Thursday morning; there were several witnesses to the fall. Reporters found that by Thursday noon, all five of the trade ministers, who had attended the Wednesday meeting, had already left town on scheduled morning flights.

Both State Senators Larry Trump and Pam Lehto confirmed that they too had met with Mr. Eda, the Governor and the trade ministers on Wednesday.

Before talking to the press Pam had called Larry, "I'm worried, Larry, I don't know if I should stir up the press, but, it's not right to keep quiet, either."

Larry replied, "But, what would you say? That Eda was murdered! By whom? And why? Wouldn't we just stir up an international squabble?

"I guess you're right," conceded Pam, "Eda must have been killed by the 'yakuza', and yet we have absolutely no proof. That is, we have no basis to make such an accusation. And our political rivals would make us look foolish if we even suggest such a thing. You know, I think that someone in that meeting must have leaked the information about the names of the 'yakuza'-owned companies being passed to the Governor on Thursday."

"Why do you say that, Pam?" Larry queried. "Couldn't the 'yakuza' have been already after him?"

"They could have, but I believe that it's just too much of a coincidence that Eda would be killed before he passed the names to Governor Hansler. The 'yakuza' was tipped off by someone in the closed meeting, but I have no idea who it might be."

"It sounds logical, but it couldn't be Ray... or you... or me, so it had to be one of the trade ministers; they sure disappeared fast."

Pam hesitated, "you know I never trusted that Italian minister, Dominic Gennero. He asked me out to dinner even after I told him I was married. Doesn't that make a difference anymore? And he asked me to go to his hotel room to discuss Italian-American trade relations. I think he meant some other kind of relations, don't you, Larry?"

Larry laughed, "I agree that he's the most logical one, but we have no proof, whatsoever, Pam. It doesn't do us any good to accuse Gennero unless we can substantiate it. The police wouldn't take a chance on arresting a foreign minister without unequivocal evidence. Think of the international implications; then we'd have both Japan and Italy mad at us."

"I guess you're right," Pam conceded, "there is absolutely nothing we can do. We'll have to let the Japanese take care of their own dirty laundry."

•

Ships passing through the narrow Rock Cut at Neebish Island were required to slow to a snail's pace to minimize the wake. This made it easier for Amos to time his plunge into the cold water and grab the rope ladder on the starboard side of the Fujima. Captain Ozeki had picked up his wet passenger at exactly 1:25 p.m. and was scheduled to pass through Lake St. Clair and the Detroit River late that evening.

Andy, exhausted after a busy morning in Lansing, was driving a rental car to Port Huron Thursday afternoon. Captain Ozeki had given him a detailed map of Lake St. Clair, which was shallow, only six feet in many areas. A narrow channel had been dredged out to allow for freighter traffic. The good Captain had selected a convenient shallow spot where Andy could wade out to the channel and swim a short distance to the Fujima.

That night, at 11:00 p.m., Amos and Andy were both relaxing in their cabin aboard the Fujima, reading about the mysterious death of the Japanese Minister of Trade, Mr. Tomizo Eda, and both smoking Havana cigars. The Fujima was heading for Lake Erie, the Welland Canal, Lake Ontario, the St. Lawrence River, the Atlantic Ocean, the Panama Canal, the Pacific Ocean and finally Tokyo, Japan. Amos and Andy were anxious to get back to their peaceful jobs in their travel agency back home.

The days following the death of Mr. Eda were hectic for the Governor's Office and the local Lansing officials. The Federal Government was frantically trying to mollify the Japanese Government over the incident. The Japanese press was accusing the Americans of every possible motive imaginable. President Barnes assured them that FBI agents were investigating the incident thoroughly. Governor Hansler was summoned to meet with the President on Friday. His State Police driver drove him to Detroit Metropolitan Airport so he could catch a direct flight to Washington.

"Look Ray, you're still my number one choice for the

Vice-Presidency, but we have to turn this mess into a favorable situation, politically. There is a lot of anti-Japan feeling, you know... the jobs thing. Just make sure that the press gets the message out that you are creating more American jobs. That can help the ticket," the President explained.

Governor Hansler related the information about the Japanese 'yakuza' to President Barnes and expressed his opinion that they were responsible for Eda's death.

"There is absolutely no evidence to support this theory, however," said the Governor. "The police have little to go on, just a broken window, apparently nothing stolen, and no witnesses. As Governor, I can't accuse a nebulous foreign organization, which is not even admitted to exist by the Japanese. We might embarrass our friends in Japan."

"Ok, then sidestep the issue. Announce your jobs agreement right away to take the heat off the murder... or accident, whichever. I'll take care of any international repercussions. And don't forget, I'm going to walk the Mackinac Bridge with you this Labor Day. But, I won't make plans until you straighten this out." President Barnes had spoken; if Governor Hansler wanted the Vice-Presidency, he knew what he had to do.

On Monday he would announce that he fully supported the construction of a Japanese-owned power-steering plant to be located in St. Johns, Michigan, just 18 miles North of Lansing. This plant would create 5,000 new American jobs. The name of the Japanese plant would be the St. Johns Manufacturing Company, which was created as a subsidiary of an old, established Japanese company, the majority interest, of which just recently passed to a newly-formed holding company. What would not be made public was that the name of that holding company was on Mr. Eda's list, a member

of the Japanese Global Trade Organization. Governor
Hansler knew, because the list was in the pocket of his
expensively tailored suit coat.

19

ON Saturday, July 18, Clayton was on duty on the Mackinaw. In the Summer the Mackinaw, the largest ice-breaker on the Great Lakes, was used somewhat as a tourist attraction. At the dock, it was open to the public during specified hours. It travelled around the Great Lakes for various reasons, none particularly urgent. Clayton would be gone for three or four days depending on the assignment.

Martha had a brainstorm on Friday afternoon, "Pam Lehto is a good friend of mine, and she was at the meeting or meetings with Mr. Eda. I'll give her a call."

State Senator Lehto told Martha that she would be driving back to Iron River early Saturday morning and could stop at Roy's cottage for a short time, probably just before noon.

Martha said, "I'll order some pasties if you will stay for lunch." Pam was persuaded.

Before Pam arrived, Martha, Luana and Roy were sitting in the dining room at the Rittenhouse table. The six foot long antique table came with the cottage because Eleanor had insisted that it be specifically mentioned in the purchase agreement. Rittenhouse furniture, made in Cheboygan, and out of production for almost thirty years, was becoming scarce and valuable.

Martha planned to return to Lansing right after Pam left for the Upper Peninsula. Martha said, "I hate to leave for fear something will happen again."

Roy assured her, "Paul Tamber will be on the night shift all week, so he'll be watching. He lives at the end of the road so he passes by frequently even when he's not on duty."

Martha was just as jealous as she was worried. She would be leaving Roy alone again with Luana. But, she remembered what Luana had said in their frank conversation, that Roy has not forgotten Eleanor, yet.

Pam Lehto arrived at 11:45 a.m. and Roy greeted her with a Finnish, that is Finglish, salutation, which sounded like, "gwinga se mena". Roy had heard Eleanor's parents and relatives use it whenever they greeted one another. Pam was too young, though; the younger generations of Finns were not learning Finnish anymore. But, she had heard the greeting many times up North and was pleased with Roy's recognition of her proud heritage.

Martha introduced Luana to Pam as a friend of Roy

and Eleanor, who was visiting Michigan for the first time, assisting Roy in his research. Pam was fascinated with Luana and wanted to talk about Hawaii whenever there was a break in the conversation, which wasn't very often. Roy had cautioned his companions that he was not going to tell anyone else about their suspicions and about the kidnapping.

Roy explained to Pam, "Martha and Luana have both been helping me with my research on the Japanese transplants in Michigan. And with the news of Mr. Eda's death we would like you to tell us whatever you can. I am concerned about what effect this accident, or perhaps murder, will have on the U.S.-Japanese auto parts war."

"Professor Nelson," Pam asked, "How much do you know about the 'yakuza'? Roy assured her that he knew about their incursion into the legitimate auto industry in general terms, but not too many specific facts.

"At the meeting with Mr. Eda, the Governor, and the five European trade ministers, and of course, Larry Trump and I were the legislative reps, Eda warned us about the 'yakuza'. We were all shocked that a Japanese diplomat would admit a weakness, but he was very disturbed. The Governor was going to meet him on Thursday, and Eda was going to give him some important information, but I can't reveal the details."

"Did he say anything about the JGTO, the Japanese Global Trade Organization?" Roy questioned.

"Why, how did you know?" Pam went on, "Mr. Eda said that it was a large association of Japanese companies in the auto parts industry, some legitimate, but some owned by the 'yakuza', and the director was a Mr...ah."

"Ito Takeda," interjected Roy.

"Right, but you seem to know what went on at the

meeting without even being there."

Roy responded, "my research has been rather revealing. See if this makes sense to you... let's put our heads
together for a minute. Mr. Eda is killed by a member of
the 'yakuza' before he gives this information, which I
guess would be the names of 'yakuza' firms, to the
Governor. But why are the names so important? These
must be the firms that will not play by the rules, and
will embarrass the legitimate Japanese firms and the
Japanese Government. Mr. Eda, who speaks for the
honest Japanese entrepreneurs, wants the Americans,
and the Europeans, to help weed out the bad seeds for
them. Otherwise, the Americans, and the Europeans
too, might just squeeze out all Japanese firms, using
tariffs and quota's. They could all gang up on the
Japanese."

Pam enthusiastically affirmed that Roy's description
was consistent with what Mr. Eda had said at the
meeting. She didn't feel that she had betrayed Mr.
Eda's trust. Roy had figured it out himself, and of
course, now Eda was dead.

"Senator Lehto," Roy added, "there is more to this
than just an economic problem. As you know, there has
been a murder, and there have been others. Someone
has even tried to kill me. We could use your help, so if
you want to join our team of amateur sleuths?"

Pam was a Swede-Finn, like Eleanor. The Swedes
conquered Finland and dominated the Western side for
some six hundred years. Some of these Western Finnish women, light blonde hair, were known to be stun-
ningly beautiful. Not Pam, her features were rugged
and her figure was athletic, not softly feminine. Her
beauty was in her erudite demeanor and the way in
which she commanded respect by her confident, yet
unobtrusive manner of handling delicate situations.

"Please call me Pam, and I'll call you Roy, if you don't mind. Yes, I would like to join your team, but you must keep me informed so I can be of help."

"I certainly don't mind, Pam, you are now a member of our informal investigating team, that makes five of us, you and I, Clayton, Martha and Luana. Martha will see to it that you are informed."

After the State Senator left, Martha said, "Pam's husband, Eino, was killed in a mine accident just one year before the Hanna Company closed the iron ore mines in Iron River. She's about our age, Roy," raising her voice a little to make sure that Luana heard her.

"She got into politics by devoting her time to getting improved working conditions in the mines. The local politicians recognized her attraction to the voters, and it has been all uphill ever since."

Martha then left for Lansing Saturday afternoon, after which Roy and Luana headed for the lawnchairs on the beach. Roy was still mentally exhausted from his ordeal. They dozed off to the peaceful lapping of the waves on the shore. That evening Roy asked Luana, "would you like to try the sauna?"

"What is it like? I've never had one; I'm afraid of all that steam," Luana explained.

"There is no steam, Luana; a sauna is very dry. When you toss water on the rocks it immediately evaporates into the air. The air in the upper level of the sauna becomes intensely hot for a few seconds. Then, after pouring water on the rocks two or three times your whole body breaks out in perspiration, your pores open up, and all the impurities, if you have any, come out. You will never feel cleaner than right after a sauna. And it's not 'saw-na', it's 'sow-na'; the advertisers on television started mispronouncing it a few years back and now everybody mispronounces it."

The sauna was about twenty feet from the cottage. It was made of beautiful Finnish pine. Their three boys had surprised Roy and Eleanor on their twenty-fifth wedding anniversary with the sauna package, which consisted of the pre-cut lumber, the electric sauna stove, the controls, and even the rocks. The complete sauna package was shipped from Finland to a distributor in Minnesota, from whom the boys had ordered it.

Roy always felt that the sauna was probably shipped on the Lotila or the Kiisla, two Finnish salties that frequently passed in front of the cottage through the Straits. Roy had built a wooden 'sauna walk' from the cottage door to the door of the sauna so you could walk barefoot.

Luana and Roy put their bathing suits on, which was not Finnish custom. He certainly didn't enjoy taking a sauna in a bathing suit, and he hadn't worn a suit in the sauna since before he and Eleanor were married, but he didn't want Luana to take her sauna alone. He wanted to show her the ropes.

Roy was relieved that Luana had a conservative suit, with a short skirt.

"I'm glad you're not in those Miss Honolulu and Miss America contests today," he opined.

"I'm so sick of seeing those seven foot tall contestants in those new style women's bathing suits that make them look like long legged ostriches or giraffes. All you see is legs and bare bottoms," Roy exaggerated.

Luana ignored his generation gap frustration and said, "it is hot," when Roy poured the first ladle of water on the rocks.

"Here," Roy handed her a wet washcloth to cover her face. Eleanor always had a bucket of cold water with a wash cloth to protect her from the wave of heat that flashed through every corner of the sauna as the water hit the rocks. It didn't bother Roy; he sometimes stood up to get the hotter waves at the top levels.

Roy kept the temperature lower than usual so that Luana wouldn't be discouraged. As the two sat on the benches, the Federal Thames, a 730 foot 'salty', registered in Cyprus, passed under the Bridge and in front of the cottage. Roy and his boys had assembled the sauna so that the front door, which had a narrow glass window, faced the Straits.

"Eleanor loved sitting here and watching the ships go by," Roy reminisced. "I think it's nice that you can enjoy it too, Luana."

He turned his head as this thought brought tears to his eyes. Roy found that whenever his enjoyment of Luana's company made him think of Eleanor, he felt like crying. He tried not to always think about her, but he couldn't stop.

"I can imagine that she must have loved her sauna very much." Noticing that Roy choked a little when he thought of Eleanor, Luana tried to be humorous, "but I'll bet you two didn't have to wear bathing suits."

Roy recovered quickly from his nostalgia and they both kept the conversation light and humorous for the rest of the evening. After the sauna, they watched "Murder She Wrote" and the late news and retired to their respective bedrooms.

20

ROY picked the late afternoon Detroit paper on Monday, July 19. The headline in the business section read, "Governor Hansler Pushes Plant in St. Johns to Employ 5,000." The article gave more details about the plant and its advantages to the community and to the State. This reminded Roy of the events of the past weeks. He and Luana were trying to reconstruct the movements of his adversaries.

"It looks as if one kidnapper, the one named Shindo, must have left the Fujima before it reached Mackinac. At least, he wasn't at the Island with those other two.

What if he left the Fujima at Chicago, flew to Lansing, killed Eda and disappeared again," Roy speculated.

"Only those eight people, the five trade ministers, the two State Senators, including Pam, and the Governor, knew that Mr. Eda was to pass the names to the Governor at noon on Thursday. Someone, who else but Governor Hansler, had to alert Shindo so that he could kill Eda before noon."

Luana added, "Shindo must have been the envoy who went to the Governor's Office after the murder. He was probably reporting to the Governor that he completed his mission. If they didn't kill Eda, everyone at the meeting would know that the Governor had the names of the 'yakuza' companies. Now it is assumed that the Governor doesn't have the names, so he doesn't have to reveal them."

"But, added Roy, "Shindo must have given him the names, after taking the list from Eda. That is why he went to the Office. So the Governor is free to support this new Japanese transplant which is probably 'yakuza'-owned. Just what Mr. Eda wanted to stop."

"Can't we tell the whole story to the press now?" Luana wondered.

"I am afraid that if I don't have convincing evidence it may backfire. That is, in an election year it may sound as if we are trying to dig up dirt. This is the time when political mudslinging brings out some weird accusations, and...well...this is so bizarre that it would probably be dismissed as a political ploy. Remember what happened in the Congressional hearings for the appointment of Judge Thomas to the Supreme Court. When it's one person's word against another, the benefit of the doubt did and should go to the accused. A person is innocent until proven guilty. We have to wait until we have an airtight case, before accusing anyone, especially a Governor, who may be running for Vice-President of the United States."

Luana had no reason to disagree with Roy, but she was concerned over his safety. They both knew that his assailants would continue pursuing him, and perhaps her, too, if their purpose was to shut them up. Amos and Andy knew when they tied her up in the cottage that she must know what is going on.

Luana suggested, "I should get back by Wednesday to judge the Annual Hula Contest in Honolulu. It begins on Friday, but I have to attend several meetings with the other judges before the contest begins. Why don't you come with me? Now, before you say no, listen! If you stay here, they will probably continue to try to kidnap or kill you. If you and I catch that late flight tonight out of Pellston, they won't figure out what happened to you for several days. In that time you can talk to Robert again, in person, and you'll be under his protection."

Roy had to admit that it was a good idea. He was supposed to be working on his research, instead of teaching this Summer, so he was free to travel. And he had accumulated 30,000 miles on United Airlines, which would give him a free round trip. He already had the coupons, so he could use them without advance reservation, but only on standby. Luana, who was a model for their Hawaiian advertisements, had unlimited complimentary passes on United Airlines. By leaving on the late Pellston flight, they would have no trouble with standby on a flight which would leave Chicago at 3:00 a.m. As soon as Roy agreed, Luana called her Mother to meet them at the airport.

•

The flight from Chicago to Honolulu took from eight to nine hours, depending on the wind velocity. Luana knew some of the Aloha crew. She had worn her mumu, anticipating the weather in Honolulu, and looked like one of them. The Hawaiian female flight attendants wore Hawaiian mumus and the men wore aloha shirts. Luana had a first class seat. Roy's ticket was economy, but she managed to have him seated beside her, the 3:00 a.m. flight was only half booked. After watching the inflight movie, Luana fell asleep and kept falling over on Roy's shoulder. Roy pulled up the middle arm rest so it wouldn't stick in her back. She ended up with her head in his lap and her feet tucked up on her seat. Roy could never sleep on these flights, but he periodically dozed off for a few minutes at a time. He enjoyed stroking Luana's soft, flowing hair and thinking again that it would have been nice if he and Eleanor had a little girl. He loved his three boys and wouldn't want it any other way, but he would always wonder.

21

ON Tuesday, at the Governor's Mansion on Mackinac Island, Hilda and Ito Takeda were arguing. "You bungled a simple job of merely bringing that professor to me," Hilda charged.

"It wasn't our fault, we got him to the Island at your request. We could have easily dumped him into Lake Michigan tied him to an anchor, but you wanted to find out what he knew about you and your brother. Wilhelm was mainly responsible once we got him here," Takeda countered.

Hilda defended her actions, "I was convinced that we

had eliminated every single person who knows about my brother and me, except you Japanese, of course."

"And only a small, privileged group of my countrymen know," Takeda assured her.

She continued, "Now I am convinced by his actions that this professor stumbled unto the secret that only Makinen and Martin could have known. I had to find out exactly what he knows, and I still want to find out. William would have convinced him to talk. And now, he will be on guard; but you still have to eliminate both of them, the professor and that Hawaiian girl. Have you found out who she is?"

"She appears to be his girlfriend. She was a beauty queen almost twenty years ago, according to my sources, so she's not as young as she looks. We just have to assume that whatever he knows, she knows too," Takeda responded.

Hilda changed the subject, "well, we kept our part of the bargain. My brother paved the way for your company to build the plant in Michigan. It's a good thing you have that State Senator on your payroll. I asked Raymond why he didn't call me about the meeting with Eda. He said it would be too risky for the Governor to be involved. We caused a lot of commotion, but it was worth it. If Eda had been alive when Raymond made the announcement about your company, he would have known right away that my brother was cooperating with the 'yakuza'."

"There is no doubt about that, which is adequate reason for disposing of Mr. Eda. By the way, one of the JGTO members wants to open another plant, to assemble windshield-wiper motors, in Grayling," Takeda informed Hilda for the first time. We would like the Governor to announce his support for this plant just before the bridge walk on Labor Day."

"That's up to him; we have already kept our word. You didn't say anything about this in our original agreement. If you try to build too many plants in one state the buy-American public will become antagonistic. And if the Governor supports another Japanese-owned auto parts factory the opposing party legislators and the press will accuse him of being responsible for the collapse of the American-owned auto parts industry," Hilda argued.

"You need us, Fraulein, if we expose you and your brother, his political career is ended. So I am afraid you will have to cooperate with us. Of course, we will let him become the candidate for Vice-President before he makes the Grayling announcement."

Hilda was tempted to have William break Takeda's neck. But, he had assured her that if anything happened to him his partners in the JGTO would take revenge; they would not hesitate in sending Fuchida and Shindo. What Hilda didn't know was that Takeda was the only one in Japan who knew about their sinister Nazi parentage. In his previous high-level government position Takeda had obtained information from classified reports. After his curiosity was raised he interviewed eye-witnesses who verified the fact that Hitler and Eva Braun had two children, and that an attempt was made to send them out of Berlin to safety.

Only Takeda had gathered all of this information and had finally traced the whereabouts of Hilda. She was active in Nazi causes, making her easier to trace. But Takeda would never have discovered her brother's identity. Hansler had no connection, whatsoever, with Nazi or even liberal causes. In the public eye he was a staunch conservative. Hilda supplied his identity in order to make the deals with Takeda and his 'yakuza' partners. Takeda let Hilda think that a small group of his crime partners, the Central Committee of the Japanese Global Trade Organization, knew all about her and her brother's heritage in order to protect himself.

Hilda and Takeda didn't trust each other, but they both needed the other in order to achieve their long range goals. Takeda and the JGTO wanted to control the auto parts industry, first in Japan and the Pacific Rim countries, then in the U.S., and finally in Europe. The U.S. was the easiest target because of its gullibility when it came to Japanese business practices. So Hilda became the key, because of her brother, to capturing the U.S. market.

Hilda had plans to manipulate her brother when he became Vice-President. In fact, Hilda visualized her brother as President, with her in control. She already had a plan formulated in her mind for the unfortunate accident which would befall President Barnes when he and Vice-President Hansler walked the Mackinac Bridge next year on Labor Day. The President had already promised her brother that he would walk the bridge this year, the first time any President of the United States will ever have walked the Mackinac Bridge. The people, especially the restaurant and motel owners, in Mackinaw Village and St. Ignace were already getting excited about the President's visit. It would be great publicity for the resort area, already a favorite of the Midwesterners.

Takeda said, "I must go back to Tokyo tomorrow. Take care of the professor as you please, it is your problem. I will be back in Lansing in two or three weeks for some legal arrangements concerning the new plant." Takeda took a small commuter flight to Pellston another to Chicago and then off to Tokyo.

Hilda said to William, after Takeda had left, "this time there must be no bungling. The professor and that

Hawaiian girl must be removed. If you need help, get Axel, he owes me a favor."

Axel was a Nazi follower who worshipped Hilda. They lived together when they were both active in the Chicago demonstrations. Hilda continued to keep in touch with him, whenever she visited Chicago. He knew about Hilda's background and would do anything she asked for the cause.

22

ROY and Luana's plane circled past Barber's Point and aimed for the Honolulu Airport runway. There on the hill was massive Tripler Hospital in its pink splendor. Roy had just read the book by Gordon Prange, "December 7, 1941, the Day the Japanese Attacked Pearl Harbor". In it he learned that there was a Tripler Hospital in front of Fort Shafter at the time of the attack. It served the Pacific war veterans throughout the war. The new, much larger, Tripler Hospital was built right after the war a few miles from Fort Shafter.

Tamar greeted them at the gate with the traditional kisses and, of course, a lei for each of them. She said, "Professor, I have some good news. My neighbors are on the mainland for two months and the house is empty. I called them and they would be delighted if you would housesit for as long as you are here. We always watch each other's place so I have a set of keys."

Roy thanked Tamar for her thoughtfulness; he hadn't even thought about where he was going to stay, it all happened so fast.

Luana said, "Thank you Mother, you are so helpful." But Tamar noticed the slight dip in Luana's head, and the almost inaudible emphasis on "help" in her last word.

Luana expected Roy to stay at her place. Her first reaction was disappointment, but now, she was actually relieved. After all, this was only a sort of business arrangement, she rationalized. She didn't like being tempted all the time; and although she would plead innocent to the charge, she was getting a little too careless at the cottage about covering herself. She embarrassed Roy a few times and apologized for her indiscretion. He was naive enough to think that sweet Luana would never do such a thing on purpose. And maybe he was right.

Luana's apartment was on Ala Moana Boulevard not too far from the Hawaiian Hilton and Ft. DeRussey, the Army quarters, probably on the most expensive property anywhere for a military installation, on the ocean at Waikiki. Tamar drove a 1984 Chevrolet, not in the best of shape. She dropped Luana off, who was too drowsy to do any more than shake Roy's hand, kiss her Mother, and say goodnight.

Tamar lived on Waimanalo Beach. Roy and Eleanor had often gone there to relax and swim in the ocean.

The tourists never ventured as far as Waimanalo; it was strictly a Hawaiian town. The house next door to Tamar was no mansion, nor was Tamar's. But each lot on the ocean was worth a million dollars or more. In front of the humble houses was an endless stretch of white sand beach. On the left it went along past the beach park at the site of now closed Bellows Air Force Base, to Kailua. Looking past Kailua you could see Mokapu Point, site of the Marine Air Corps Station and the Red-footed Booby Colony. On the right the beach stretched past some small beach parks, past the beach house where Magnum, P.I. was filmed, to Sea World Park and Makapuu Point.

Roy had no trouble making himself at home in the neighbor's beach house. It was owned by a Hawaiian couple in their thirties. She worked as a naturalist at Foster Botanic Gardens. An interesting, but as Tamar said, a low paying job. Her husband never grew up from being a beach bum; he worked off and on in construction. He had a chance to work on a job in Los Angeles for two-months and she tagged along for a vacation.

Roy never suffered from jet lag. He was able to adjust to the change in time easily after one good sleep. He relaxed on the beach, but under the shade of the palm trees, most of Wednesday.

Luana called him late Thursday morning "Roy, I am at the Honolulu Convention Center, remember, the Neal S. Blaisdell Center, you know where it is don't you? Our meeting will be over at noon."

Roy picked up Luana's subtle hint. He hadn't called her since they arrived, assuming that she would be busy with her meetings. "Would you like to have lunch with me and take a drive around the Island?" Roy asked.

"I'll be waiting at the main entrance at noon," she

replied.

From Waimanalo, it seemed quicker for Roy to drive around the South shore, past Sunny Beach, a favorite of the surfers, through Hawaii Kai, a development of Henry J. Kaiser, and along Highway H1 to Kapiolani Street. The Blaisdell Convention Center was almost downtown, at the corner of Kapiolani and Ward Avenue.

Luana was waiting at the main entrance. She was in a business suit. A light blue silk Jacket and slacks with a delicate white blouse and a rose scarf. Her hair was drawn up tight in a bun. She looked confident and authoritative. Her imposing appearance of self-assurance was intimidating to Roy; just what he didn't like in a woman.

If Roy had a weakness, it was in his relationships with women. Aggressive, beautiful women made him feel inferior. Eleanor was a striking blonde Finnish beauty, but she was timid. In the leading studies of the Finns it is generalized that Finnish people underrate themselves. They are generally introverted and reticent, in spite of the fact that they are highly prepared and qualified. Pretty, but humble, Eleanor fit Roy's need for someone to depend on him.

Roy just adored the Hawaiian women because of these same humble qualities. In her auspicious business suit, Luana was no longer the meek little Hawaiian girl. It challenged Roy's image of her. For the first time he realized that she was a capable, self-assured, independent person. Not like the dependent Eleanor, who thrived on letting Roy drive her everywhere and whose life centered around her husband. His successes were hers; she didn't publish or teach college; she raised three children and was a homemaker. She and Roy loved it; they were happy doing everything together.

"You'd better change your clothes, I'll drive you to your apartment." Roy said somewhat presumptuously.

"Don't you want to have lunch first? Luana replied, slightly irritated. "Didn't you notice my new outfit?

"Oh! Yes, you look very nice."

Luana thought, "this from a college professor, whose choice of colorful, esoteric, descriptive words was one of his discriminating characteristics."

Luana began to sense the uneasiness, but she would never be able to understand the complexity of Roy's feelings. She was hurt by his blatant disinterest in her new outfit, and by his nonchalant attitude.

During her flight to Michigan, she had noticed how different the mainland was from the Islands. She had a two-hour wait at O'Hare Airport in Chicago. She watched all of the businesswomen in their pin-stripe suits with shirt and tie, just like the men. She couldn't believe that even in July they wore navy blue suits. By contrast, she had left the Honolulu crowd in their mumus and their aloha shirts.

She had deliberately purchased her new outfit, assuming that Roy would finally notice her and see her as a mature, capable woman. So his reaction, or nonreaction, was an irritation to her.

Roy drove her to her apartment. Luana changed to her casual clothes, a mumu, and let her hair down from the tight bun she had worn with her suit. Roy waited in the car.

When she came down he said, "now, that's a pretty dress, is it new?

Luana didn't respond to his compliment. It was an old mumu; but, perhaps she had never worn it in Roy's company. He made these pleasant, noncommittal remarks to her frequently, and she couldn't quite understand them.

Roy had been in the habit of doing this to other women when he was with Eleanor, and he continued just as if she were still alive. During their marriage he had admired and became good friends with many women at various times. He made it a point never to make remarks of a personal or flirtatious nature. If a woman friend of Eleanor's were ravishingly beautiful, Roy would merely say that she had a pretty dress or something neutral. He would never say that she was beautiful.

He was now doing the same thing with Luana. He wanted to say, "Luana you are the sweetest girl in the world," but he just couldn't. He had never been personal with any other woman, except his wife. Even in their courtship, which lasted three years, they never acquiesced to their physical urges for a closer relationship. Instead, they were married in Roy's senior year at college, rather than pursue what they both considered an immoral solution. So Roy's intimate personal compliments were reserved for only one woman. And he hadn't let go of that woman, yet.

"I want to take you the Yum Yum Tree in Kailua." He stopped himself before he said it was one of Eleanor's favorite places.

"And then we will drive around the Island. How does that sound, you don't have any more meetings today, do you?

"It sounds wonderful. I hate to admit it, but I have never been to the Yum Yum in Kailua, just the one at Ward Center."

They drove back through Waimanalo along the ocean to Kailua and had lunch. Roy had Mahi Mahi, his favorite, and Luana had a more delicate entree. Roy had selected this restaurant because of the ducks. It was situated on a canal and there was always a family of baby ducklings following their mother around. Today was no exception. Luana enjoyed them just as much as Roy did.

They drove up the coast to the park at Chinaman's Hat, a tiny island in the shape of a hat, and past the Crouching Lion, a natural formation in the hillside. Next they came to the Polynesian Cultural Center at Laie, the most authentic tourist attraction on Oahu, thought Roy. It was also the site of Brigham Young University at Hawaii and the Mormon Temple. Roy had been given a tour of the University and tickets to the show by the Chairman of the Accounting Department a few years back. The students at the University were mainly Polynesians from Hawaii, Fiji, Tonga, the Marquesas, New Zealand, Tahiti and Samoa.

He and Luana had both been there before so they drove on to the Kahuku Sugar Mill. The sugar mill, now closed for economic reasons, is located at the Northern tip of Oahu. The mill had been made into a tourist attraction with souvenir shops in the old buildings. There was a catwalk over the huge grinding machines which turned the sugar cane into sugar. The two walked over the catwalk and around the back to the tourist shops.

Only the experienced surfers dare challenge the monstrous waves in the Winter months at Sunset Beach. It was July so the waves were behaving for the young service men and women from Schofield Barracks and the other military bases nearby, who were bathing and surfing on the North Coast beaches. Roy drove through Wahiawa to the Dole Pineapple Welcome Center where they had a dish of Pineapple Sherbet.

He and Luana stopped in the parking lot to gaze at Kolekole Pass, a 1,700 foot high dip in the 3,000 foot mountains, through which the Japanese bombers, fighters and torpedo planes passed on their ominous flight to Pearl Harbor. The sight of Kolekole Pass always gave Roy an eerie feeling, the same feeling he had when he stood on the Arizona Memorial. It was the only time in his life he felt the presence of ghosts or spirits. Standing on the Arizona seemed to awaken the spirits of the 1,102 sailors entombed in the watery grave below. They drove on toward Pearl City and back to Honolulu. It was only about 90 miles around the Island. There was a lot more to see on the circle drive, but they both had seen enough for one day.

Luana said, "that was fun, Roy. You know, I've lived here all my life, but I haven't taken time to really appreciate the sights you showed me today. Thank you."

"Good," Roy was excited, "next time we'll stop to see Byodo-In Temple, and let's go to Foster Gardens, I want to show you the Cannon Ball Tree and the Mindendao Gum Tree; those are my two favorites." Foster Botanic Gardens had an assortment of tropical trees not seen on the mainland, and several were the largest of their species in America.

He paused, "Oh, but you've probably seen it. Here, I've been acting like a tourist guide and you were born and raised here."

Roy was treating her like Eleanor again. When he first taught in Hawaii, at the Education Center at Tripler Army Hospital, he came over alone for the first sixteen days. Eleanor flew over to join him for the last two weeks. He was like a little kid showing her all the interesting places he had discovered.

Luana said politely, "I've never really taken time to see it. I'd love to go with you sometime. She reminded him, "now remember, I'm judging the Hula Contest starting Friday noon until Saturday about 10 o'clock. You will be able to get in free anytime you want. I'll inform the gate committee that you're my guest. I will have a break for dinner on Friday at six, that is... well, I shouldn't always presume that..."

"You're not presuming anything, Luana, you know that while I'm here I am entirely at your... well, it never dawned on me, but, maybe I'm imposing on you," Roy said.

"No, of course not." Luana was relieved that they straightened that out, they were both too clumsy with their apologetics. I'll wait in the judging booth for you at six tomorrow, Ok?" Luana stated.

They were both worn out, but hungry so they just grabbed a snack at Bob's, the only Big Boy restaurant in Hawaii, and probably the only Big Boy that served teriyaki sauce on the famous Big Boy hamburger.

Roy dropped Luana off at her apartment and drove back to Waimanalo. He stopped in to visit with Tamar. Shortly after he was settled in the house next door to Tamar, Roy had called Clayton to give him Tamar's telephone number.

"Your friend, Clayton, called and wants you to call back as soon as you can," she told Roy.

It was after midnight in Michigan, so Roy waited until early Friday morning to call Clayton. Clayton said, "Roy, this strictly confidential. Governor Hansler called yesterday; he wants you to meet with him in Lansing on Monday. He gave me a telephone number for you to call him at 9:00 a.m. He said that he would tell you where to meet him then. I didn't say where you were. I just said that I will give you the message. He was very formal about it, and so was I."

Roy asked Clayton if he would mind picking him up at the Pellston Airport on Sunday, and to give him the number then.

•

Roy went to the Hula Competition at 4:00 p.m. He could see Luana in the Judging area. She wore her most native Hawaiian costume, a hand sewn mumu with fresh purple and white leis around her neck and a wide brimmed straw hat with a colorful scarf around the brim. She was dressed like the Tutu-ladies, the grand-mothers who went around to the area schools teaching the young Hawaiians the native customs and dances.

Roy was amazed by the chanters. There were even different categories of the ancient Polynesian chants, which date back to the the time when the Polynesians had no written language. The contestants stood in the center of the convention center and, with no micro-phone, chanted to the delight of the audience. There were also two main Hula dancing categories. Roy could only describe them as slow, like the Hawaiians in long formal mumus, and fast, like the Grass skirted Tahi-tians.

The next performance he watched was a group of little girls from Tokyo. Almost all of the competitors in the two-day contest were from Hawaii, but a few were from Japan and other Pacific Islands. The Japanese girls, about forty of them, were the only group in which the performers were all exactly the same height, about 4 feet, eight inches tall; so Roy just assumed that they were all about ten to twelve years old. After their performance it was time for the 6:00 o'clock dinner break. The Japanese performers were mingling with the audience as Roy made his way toward the judging stands where he was to meet Luana. To his amazement the Japanese performers were not little girls, but women in their 30's, 40's and some 50 or more in age.

The Ward Warehouse and Ward Center were full of specialty shops and good restaurants and were just a few blocks away. Roy loved Horatio's and Orson's fresh catch, which was one of the local fish, Mahi-mahi, Opakapaka, Ahi, Ulua or Ono. He decided on Orson's for the view. The seating allowed the diner to see the lush, green mountains on one side, and the deep blue ocean, with six foot waves splashing white foam on the other side. Roy wanted this evening to be special because he knew that this would be his last dinner with Luana for a while. He would leave for Lansing tomorrow.

After they finished eating Roy informed her of his plans, "Luana, I have to leave for Lansing tomorrow afternoon. Governor Hansler called Clayton and requested that I meet him on Monday."

Luana was disappointed, but she knew that it had to be important, "What did Clayton say, did the Governor explain why he wants to see you?"

"No, he just left a message because Clayton wouldn't tell anyone where we are. The meeting is on Monday. I think I'll fly to Pellston instead of Lansing. I'll get there on Sunday morning, rest up, and drive to Lansing. I'll call Martha and see if I can stay overnight with her, she has a large house. Do you think she'll mind?"

"Of course not," Luana assented out of sheer gentility. Her feminine instincts wanted her to say, "No, it would be in bad taste to stay overnight in Martha's house." Would Roy be as much of a gentleman with Martha, as he was with her?

But Luana remained a perfect lady. "Whoops, it's time to get back, we have two more hours. I want to see you off tomorrow, but I can't. The contest is on all day

Saturday."

Roy drove Luana back to the main entrance of Blaisdell Center. They stood nervously in front of the building for a few seconds before Luana blurted out, "I don't know how to say this, Roy, but I...I really care about you. Why do you think I'm willing to be with you almost all my free time? Why would I fly all the way to Mackinaw Village? There are quite a few men right here in Honolulu who call me regularly to go out with them, and that's not all they want me to do with them. But I don't. Don't you know why? When I thought you were dead back in that awful ship, I didn't know what to do. I wanted to... oh you wouldn't understand. Roy, don't you know that I... I'm sorry, I guess I'm just terribly worried about you."

Roy was a coward. Now he knew what the Bible meant by 'temptation of the flesh.' He had never personally experienced the sensual temptation that he now had as he looked into Luana's beauteous, pleading eyes. He wanted to grab her into his arms, but he didn't. Luana turned and walked briskly away so that he wouldn't see the flood of tears that were ready to burst forth. She was ashamed of what she had blurted out, knowing that this Martha thing caused her to be jealous.

Roy didn't see Luana again before he left Honolulu. He didn't want to even think about what Luana said. He could only plead, "Oh, Eleanor, I wish I could know for sure. Where are you, Eleanor? Please let me know."

23

ROY arrived at Pellston on Sunday morning, July 26, when it was six hours later in Michigan than in Honolulu. He called Martha and of course she was delighted to have him stay overnight on Sunday. She had a guest bedroom in her spacious house. He thanked Clayton for his help and drove to Lansing on Sunday afternoon. He and Martha went to Bill Knapps for dinner and talked about their schooldays and the class reunion. Roy would love to see some of his old friends again.

Roy called the number at 9:00 a.m. on Monday and

Governor Hansler answered. He gave Roy an address of an apartment in East Lansing and asked if he could come right over. Roy drove to the rather inconspicuous looking apartment, and the Governor himself answered the door.

"How do you do, Professor Nelson," Governor Hansler greeted Roy. "I've heard a lot about your research in the auto parts industry, which is of great interest to me. We probably met at some of academic meetings, but I'm sure that I've never had the opportunity to talk individually with you."

"You are quite right, Governor Hansler," said Roy. "You were the main speaker at our last meeting in Flint. I was in the audience."

"This is a more delicate matter," the Governor continued. "I know what has happened to you, and I am very sorry."

Roy was a little confused at this statement. Did he mean that no one paid any attention to his warnings about the Japanese booting the U.S. auto parts suppliers around, or did he mean something else.

"This room," he continued seriously, "is completely private. There are no recording devices. This conversation is for you alone, please don't even tell your other friends who are working with you."

"You have my word, Governor, as long as it doesn't conflict with the safety of any one of them or me."

"When I was about twelve, my parents, who were wonderful, kind people, told me that I was adopted. Now, I knew it in a child's way, but they waited until I was old enough to understand what it meant to be adopted."

The Governor stopped and asked, "would you like a drink, Roy?"

Roy, seeing the coffee pot said, "I'd love some coffee."

They both had a cup of coffee and the conversation continued, the Governor a little more relaxed.

"My parents were careful to explain every detail. In 1945, when I was five, a German woman brought me to America and made arrangements for my adoption through legal channels. She had papers saying that my German parents were killed in the war. The Hanslers were second generation German-Americans. They were in their late thirties and had no children. My father, Mr. Hansler, that is, worked during the war as an electrician at the Willow Run bomber plant."

The Governor continued his story, "I led a perfectly normal life in high school. No one considered me any different from the typical, normal American boy. I went to Wayne University, majoring in Political Science, expecting to go to law school. But instead I later went to Michigan State for an MBA. Let's see, that was about 1975. My career always seemed to lead me into politics, until, as you know, I became successful. I'm sure you must know that 90% of it is just pure luck. You have to be in the right place at the right time."

They stopped for a minute to replenish their coffee cups and the Governor went on, "shortly after my second term as Governor a mysterious woman insisted in making an appointment with me, claiming that it was a personal matter. She was very insistent that we have complete privacy, for my sake, she said. It was as if she were the mother of a pregnant daughter who claimed me as the father. But her story was quite different."

The Governor went on, "she said 'I'm your sister', just like that, 'I'm your sister'. She told me that her name was Hilda Schwartz and that she was taken to Aylmer, Ontario, Canada by the wife of a German prisoner of war, Emil Schwartz. Aylmer is just north of St. Thomas and not far from London, Ontario. German prisoners were put to work in the fields in Southern Ontario, the breadbasket of Canada. She said they later moved to the U.S. Her parents told her of her wonderful Nazi heritage. She became an avid follower of the fascist movement in America, following her father, who was one of the leaders."

Governor Hansler hesitated for a few seconds, as if to brace himself for the next part, "she told me that on her eighteenth birthday, her mother and father did a strange thing. Her mother prepared an elaborate sauerbraten dinner; the table had lace doilies with fancy candlesticks, and she had baked and decorated a birthday cake. Hilda said that her parents had always been frugal and austere and had never fussed over her before. They made it a kind of celebration. When they finished dinner and her mother passed out the cake, her father said, 'happy birthday, Hilda, daughter of Adolph Hitler, long live the Fuhrer's daughter."

Governor Hansler became animated in expressing, "I was, of course, shocked and I blurted out, "you mean that..."

"Yes, Hilda said to me, 'it means that you are the only son of Adolph Hitler. But, no one must know. Our parents are the only ones who knew, and they are all dead, now."

The Governor went on, "after the shock wore off, although the horror of it never has worn off, I had to be realistic. It didn't take much to realize that this woman was a fanatic Nazi lover, but she was probably right about me. Everything she said made sense about our background. You see, I do vaguely remember having a little sister."

He continued, "but, it became apparent to me that I could not reveal my parentage. It would be the end of my political career, any career, for that matter. If there is one person in the world who would be voted the most likely not to be forgiven by Americans and Europeans, it would be Adolph Hitler, don't you agree?"

"I have to agree, but it sounds as if you are saying that you had no Nazi leanings at all. Does that mean that you are not working with her in all this harassment that I've been going through," Roy wondered out loud.

"Well, yes and no," the Governor vacillated. "I have been cooperating with Hilda and Takeda, but out of necessity. If I don't cooperate they will expose me and my life will be ruined. If I do cooperate, I may possibly be able to fight back somehow, someday. And now, I may have my chance."

"What's that," Roy wondered.

"You...you are my only hope to destroy them, without exposing my identity. You are the first person I have told my story to, because I know that you will understand. Your life has been threatened, and they will keep on trying to kill you. You know the truth and they know it. I believe...I'm afraid that they even killed my parents. Can you imagine the cold blooded fanatic she must be to have my parents murdered. And I can't do a thing about it."

"I want to believe you, but how about your announcement after you knew which Japanese companies were on that list. And how about the murder of Mr. Eda? You had to inform Hilda and her murderous 'yakuzas' about the list."

"No, I didn't. One of the two State Senators must have done it, because I didn't," the Governor sounded convincingly sincere.

"But the announcement, ... I have to admit I was a political coward. The President wanted me to create jobs to look good on the ticket and how could I expose the 'yakuza' connection? If I did, those at the closed meeting would know that I had the list. But, I wasn't supposed to have received the list, since my meeting with Eda was at noon, and he jump...was pushed out of the window at 10 something. Shindo brought the list to my office, at the beckoning of Hilda, straight from the hotel where he killed Eda."

Roy was alarmed because he thought so much of Pam, "You think that a State Senator could be on the payroll of the 'yakuza'?"

The Governor opined after weighing the question carefully, "It could very well be an innocent arrangement, since the JGTO is only partially owned by the 'yakuza'. The relationship could be legal. But, under the circumstances, not too ethical, considering that everyone in that closed meeting with Trade Minister Eda gave his word not to reveal what Eda said. And everyone present understood that there was a potential danger to Eda if the 'yakuza' found out."

At this point the Governor's voice exuded sincerity, "Roy, would you help me try to stop these traitors, Hilda and Takeda. It requires our complete secrecy; it will be dangerous, and there will never be any credit given to you or any knowledge that you served your country in one of the most heroic efforts ever."

"You see, we can't tell anyone. We can't get help from the police or the FBI. It is ironic, isn't it? Here I am the titular head of the State of Michigan with the entire State Police Force and the National Guard at my command in case of riots and tornados, but I can't even get help for myself."

"My first loyalty is to my country and I would make a conscientious, effective Vice-President of the United States. But, not with Hilda calling the shots. How can we, without murdering anyone, eliminate the threat that she holds over me?"

Roy attempted to answer, "it won't be easy because she seems to live only for the Nazi cause, and she has anyone killed who stands in the way. A person like that cannot be stopped short of dying for the cause. We can't accuse her of any crime without exposing you, so it seems impossible," Roy talked himself right out of a solution.

"How does Takeda fit into all this?" Roy asked.

Governor Hansler explained, "Ito Takeda is from a wealthy Japanese industrial family, legitimate, by the way. He accidentally stumbled on some old German records, smuggled to Tokyo, from the last days in Berlin in 1945. He pursued the reference to Hitler's children until he traced Hilda. It was a natural old Axis' union. Takeda represented the Japanese 'yakuza' which desperately wanted to give the Americans another taste of Pearl Harbor, not with bombers but with economic dominance. And Hilda held the key, a way to control the Governor of Michigan, the automotive capital of the United States. I was to become the pawn of both Hilda and Takeda, and I couldn't do a thing about, except resign. And if I did they threatened to kill me anyway, since I would no longer be of value to them."

Roy said, "As you said, let's keep our alliance a secret. It may work to our advantage. I notice that you kept our meeting today rather low key. I don't think anyone except my friends know about our meeting, and my friends are trustworthy. I'm afraid they will have to be in on some of our arrangements since they know so much about what has been happening to me."

"Use your own judgment, just keep in mind that our lives... both of our lives depend on secrecy, " the Governor warned.

"What if you are not really Hilda's brother?" Roy

asked.

"Hilda claims that she has records, some signed by the Hanslers, with pictures proving that I am her brother. She showed me enough to convince me that they are authentic. I looked around her room in the Summer Residence at Mackinac several times, when she was out, but I could never find any of the records."

Roy then asked, "Governor Hansler, what happened to Professor Makinen, I must know why he disappeared, and is he dead or being held somewhere?"

"Let's start from the beginning," the Governor responded. Mrs. Schwartz apparently took the two children, my sister and me, that is, to Finland; the Nazi's were still in Finland; they didn't declare war on Germany until March of 1945. And Professor Makinen was apparently in charge of the clandestine arrangements to get us out of Europe into Canada. They had decided that I was to be separated from my sister and adopted by an American couple, which turned out to be the Hanslers, of course. Professor Makinen and only one or two others, who assisted him, knew about all the details."

He walked over to his desk. On top of the desk was a walnut Built-Rite Manufacturers' pipe-rack humidor combination, which was made in the 1950's in Detroit. He pulled out a hand-carved pipe and filled it with Prince Albert pipe tobacco. He lit the pipe and took a long first puff. "You know, these pipe racks were sold to J.L. Hudson, L.S. Ayres, Lord & Taylor, and only the most expensive department store in each big city. They are so rare that they are becoming valuable antiques " He apparently didn't want to rush his explanation of the events.

The Governor continued, "During the meeting, I guess it was in the middle of May, I met Professor

Makinen at the Grand Hotel. We talked about the long overdue honor given him by the Finnish Government, and then he asked if he could talk to me in private. We found a private room and he began. He said that my housekeeper at the Governor's Mansion was the little girl whom he assisted in leaving Finland, forty-seven years ago."

"Then he somberly explained who she was, the daughter of Adolph Hitler and Eva Braun. He said that he, and his friend in Hawaii, were the only ones left who knew about it. He knew that the little girl was to be adopted by Mrs. Schwartz and her husband, and he knew about the Schwartz's activism in the Nazi movement in America. He kept it to himself as long as it was harmless. But, when he traced Hilda to the Governor's personal staff he felt obligated to tell the Governor in confidence. There was no hint that he knew about me."

Roy offered, "I'll bet that the Hanslers were selected after Professor Makinen's part in the mission was completed and that explains why he never knew their identity."

"It must have been, because he never would have approached me if he knew that I were the son."

The Governor went on, "when my part in the meeting was over early, I returned to the Governor's Mansion, and like a fool I told Hilda about it. I just thought that she should be aware of it. I thought nothing of Hilda and William's trip into town, Mackinaw Village, that is; they went in for drinks and dinner frequently. There are few, if any, good eating and drinking places open on the Island in May.

"So when you heard that Professor Makinen disappeared on the Mackinac Bridge, you put two and two together."

The Governor added, "right, I was furious when I

read it in the paper the next day, but I was already back in Lansing. The next time I saw Hilda on Mackinac Island I demanded an explanation. She haughtily said that she would decide what is necessary to preserve our anonymity."

"Did you know about Harold Martin's murder?"

"No, Hilda and Takeda arranged that. Takeda has connections with the 'yakuza'. This Shindo, who gave me the list, and another 'yakuza' killer, named Fuchida, do all of Takeda's dirty work. They were not sure that Martin knew Hilda's identity, but knew that Dr. Makinen could have told him. They found a letter or something that made them think that he knew. They didn't tell me about it until after he was killed. I was upset, but Hilda knew that I couldn't do anything about it then. Can you understand what a trap I'm in? As long as Hilda is alive I am helpless."

It was like an appeal to get rid of Hilda, Roy thought, but he would have no part of a violent solution. There must be some way to help the Governor, but how?

Roy left the apartment first and Governor Hansler followed later. The Governor had said that he would warn Roy if Hilda made a move to have him or his friends killed by Wilhelm or the 'yakuza' team of Fuchida and Shindo. Roy had agreed to help the Governor in whatever way he could. But at the conclusion of their meeting he couldn't imagine how they were going to stop Hilda and Takeda.

The Governor's private apartment in East Lansing was near the Michigan State University campus, so Roy stopped in to see if his mentor, Professor Jones was in Eppley Center, the business school building. Dr. Jones had been his dissertation chairman and Roy always kept in touch with him. This was to be his last year as Associate Dean, so Roy wanted to chat with him about his plans after retirement. Dr. Jones' secretary informed Roy that he would be in meetings all day. Roy borrowed the phone and called Martha.

"How about lunch?"

Martha said, "do you know where Clara's is?"

Roy said, "sure, meet you there in 20 minutes. We have to talk."

Clara's restaurant was near downtown Lansing at the old, converted railroad station. Roy and Eleanor had loved the gourmet lunches and the realistic decor of the old building. For Roy the atmosphere and the seating were almost as important as the food. Oh how he hated those hosts and hostesses who seated him at a table in the middle of a crowded, noisy area, while there were empty quiet tables available. Smoke didn't bother him as much noise did, especially that from bratty children. Roy always asked for a quiet, booth or table with a view of the mountains and the ocean, even in the middle of flat Lansing. This usually got the attention of the hostess, who then jokingly described the parking lot view as if you could hear the waves splashing on the beach.

After being seated in a quiet, comfortable booth at Clara's, Roy ordered his favorite grilled chicken on a bed of rice and Martha ordered fettucini alfredo. Roy gave Martha an abbreviated version of his meeting with the Governor. "The important thing is that I have a completely different view of the Governor's loyalty. I believe now that he's an innocent victim."

"But," Martha interjected, "what if he were lying? What if is deliberately trying to throw you...us, off guard. What better way than to make up a story of being an innocent bystander. Remember that he is the one who actually caused the death of Professor Makinen by telling Hilda. He is the one who threw his support to the new 'yakuza'-owned plant. And I still think the Governor told Takeda about the list, no matter what he claims."

"I know," countered Roy, "but his explanations are believable. Martha, can you get Pam and that other senator, um... what's his name, to meet with us tonight at your place? "

"Larry Trump, I'll try."

Martha was able to get them together that night. Roy had to be tactful in approaching what had to be a puzzling question. He was hoping that Pam had nothing to do with the 'yakuza'.

After the usual chatting Roy said, "Minister Tomiza Eda didn't commit suicide or jump out of the window; he was murdered by the 'yakuza'. We have reason to believe that someone in the secret meeting with Mr. Eda informed Mr. Ito Takeda, Director of the Japanese Global Trade Organization, about the list that was to be given to the Governor. And that information lead to the murder. It could have been, although not likely, one of the European trade ministers. I don't think that it could have been the Governor. Do either of you know anything that could shed light on this?"

State Senator Larry Trump unhesitatingly said, "I'm sorry to say that I told him. But, please let me explain. I was hired by Takeda to assist in promoting the image of the JGTO in Michigan. I checked into all of the legal and ethical aspects of the relationship before I entered into a contract. However, with the possibility of legislation involving a new plant owned by a JGTO member, I asked to terminate our relationship at once, because of conflict of interest. Takeda was furious. He threatened to anonymously leak to the press that I knew all along about the legislature and that I took money to influence other legislators. It was blackmail. He seemed to know that Eda was up to something so he said he would let me off the hook if I gave him any information of significance from the secret meeting. I knew that the secret list must be what he wanted, so I told him about it after the meeting."

Pam asked, "then you told him how the list was to be passed to the Governor personally by Eda at his hotel?"

"Yes, I'm afraid so. I didn't know, or even think, they would kill Eda. I kept hoping, or maybe wishful thinking, that Eda had died accidentally. Up to the meeting I didn't even know that the 'yakuza' was involved. But it was too late. My reputation and career would be ruined if I didn't cooperate," Trump rationalized.

Roy said, "well that explains the murder of Eda. You're lucky Mr. Trump. We can't tell your connection with Mr. Eda's murder to anyone, including the police. So now your reputation and career depend on you keeping this meeting a secret. No one must know what was discussed here. Don't ask why, just keep quiet. More than your reputation is at stake, the lives of several innocent people are at stake."

Larry Trump left, obsequiously thanking them for keeping his secret, not fully aware why it served their purpose more than his.

Roy said to Martha and Pam, "well that verifies that the Governor was telling the truth. Are you convinced or not, Martha?"

"Well, maybe," Martha conceded reluctantly."

"Pam, how about you? What do you think about all this?"

"I'm disappointed in Larry, although I should have some consolation in that he's in the opposing party. I'm sure relieved that Ray Hansler is not involved.

"Pam, I know we have involved you to a great extent, but for your own safety and for your political future you should not know everything, yet. I had to ask you here today because I didn't know for sure which one of you informed Takeda. Martha was convinced that Governor Hansler did it, but I wasn't. And we were both hoping that it wasn't you. Unfortunately, you were one of the few people who could have done it, so you had to be eliminated as a possibility. I really didn't expect Larry Trump to blurt it out so readily. We were lucky in that respect."

24

THE next week, at the Republican Convention, the Governor of Michigan, Raymond Hansler, was nominated for Vice-President of the United States. Roy had spent several days in Mt. Pleasant at the University, preparing for the Fall Semester. He also researched the literature on Hitler's children. Surprisingly, he could find few references to authenticate their existence. In Roy's discussion with the Governor he had admitted that there was some doubt about Hitler having children with Eva Braun.

The Governor said that he had accused Hilda and

Takeda of making it up. But, Takeda had a report signed by Martin Bormann authorizing the transportation of two children, a boy and a girl, to Finland, which was then Germany's ally. The Governor said that the papers were authentic. Takeda also had pictures of Mrs. Schwartz and the two children in Germany and in Finland. Hilda said she recognized her mother in the photograph and had more recent photos of her mother which seemed to resemble the woman in the older picture.

Takeda explained that Hitler and Eva Braun were not married until hours before their death in 1945. The children were born out of wedlock and, in 1939 and 1940, Eva Braun was not respectable enough for Hitler to be seen with her in public. In fact, Eva was seldom seen with him at important, official functions until 1945. Eva was afraid that Hitler would have her children killed. He became a megalomaniac about the 'superior race' and he believed that Eva had a Jewish grandparent. Eva was deathly afraid that he would have her children killed, because he said that they were not only 'bastards', but 'Jewish bastards'. He would scream this at her when he went into one of his maniacal rages.

The children were taken by Eva's sister to Sweden in 1941 and the children remained there until early 1945. Eva's sister, wife of a prominent Nazi, returned to Berlin. In 1945, knowing that the end was coming, Hitler married Eva to make the children legitimate. He had a complete change of heart, knowing that he was going to die. He had already planned his and Eva's suicide. Eva sent for the children and they arrived in Berlin. But it became unsafe with the bombing and the impending invasion, so they were sent to Finland instead, where they would be safe. And from there Mrs.

Schwartz took them to Canada and the U.S.

The Governor believed the story, even though it came from Hilda and Takeda, because there were other official sources which seemed to verify it. The story in the June 25, 1945 issue of Life Magazine stated that Swedish sources verified the existence of two children, a boy and a girl.

Roy concluded, however, that there was still a possibility that it was all a hoax, so that Takeda, and the 'yakuza' could control the man who was most likely to become the next Vice-President of the greatest nation in the world.

•

On Monday, August 10, Roy drove from Mt. Pleasant to Mackinaw to the cottage. He and Clayton went to Darrow's Restaurant for dinner. Roy updated Clayton on what had happened and what he had learned in Lansing. Roy was no longer worried about being abducted because he believed that the Governor would warn him if any dirtywork were being planned by Hilda or Takeda.

On Tuesday morning, Roy received a call from Governor Hansler. "Professor Nelson... Roy, I am going to be at the Mansion later today. I have a plan to trap Hilda and Takeda, but I need your help. It may be dangerous, so don't hesitate to say no. If you want to help me, be at the Mansion at nine o'clock sharp tonight. You must come alone and don't let anyone see you. Wait on the porch until I get you."

Roy replied, "I'll be there. I want to solve this dilemma as much as you do. I can't rest until the threat that hangs over my life is over. See you there tonight."

Clayton promised to stay in the shadows, but would not agree to let Roy go alone. He and Roy took off in the Nicolet at 8:15 for Mackinac Island. Clayton docked his venerable Chris Craft and Roy started out alone. Clayton agreed to wait one-half hour and then start out in the opposite direction from the Governor's Mansion. When he reached the center of town, he would turn up the hill and come around to the Mansion from the West. He would remain in the thick bushes on the hill below the house.

Roy climbed Fort Street, the steep narrow path beside Fort Mackinac, and approached the Governor's Mansion. He walked quietly up to the front porch. The hillside porch had a panoramic view of the harbor and the Straits. There was a steep drop from the edge of the porch, with a rock formation at the bottom of the hill. The wide French doors leading to the porch were open so that Roy could hear voices coming from the living room. He stopped to listen.

It was Governor Hansler's voice; he seemed to be shouting, "you two kidnap him, drag him all over the Great Lakes and then you let him go without a scratch. All I had to do was call him and he is on his way. Now, stay out of sight until I give you the signal to come in. Then Wilhelm can dispose of him. You two bungled the job, so I'll have to finish it for you. I had to take care of the Eda problem, too. I told the Professor that I was a poor, innocent bystander, that I didn't know about the Fuhrer being my father. He believed everything, what a fool! So he'll be here, don't you worry. Go ahead now. He should be here any minute."

Roy was shocked by what he heard. He wanted to turn and run when he stumbled on a wicker porch chair. The Governor stepped outside on the porch and saw Roy.

"Oh, there you are, Roy. Come on in." The Governor seemed to deliberately control the conversation, so that Roy couldn't ask any questions. He talked about the convention and his nomination. He regretted having to step down as Governor, but looked forward to the challenge in Washington. Roy was especially uneasy, knowing that at any minute he might be killed. He wasn't listening to the Governor at all, just planning how he could get word to Clayton for help.

The Governor walked to an inside door and motioned. Ito Takeda and Hilda walked in. Roy could see Wilhelm standing in the other room as the door swung open and closed again.

Hilda said, "We finally caught you, Mr. Professor. Now you are going to tell us how much you know willingly, or Wilhelm will help you to remember."

"He knows everything, I can assure you," said Hansler.

Hilda growled, "but who else knows? We must find out and kill them too."

Takeda agreed. "Now that the Governor will become Vice-President, we have more at stake. His identity must be protected at all costs. We know about the Hawaiian girl. I have already talked to Captain Ozeki. He will drop our two friends off in Honolulu on Wednesday or Thursday to take care of her. Her name is Luana Kameha and she dances at one of the hotels. They will find her easily. We also know that our dear professor's neighbor, a man named Clayton LaCombe, knows too much. Fuchida and Shindo will take care of him after they leave Honolulu. And finally, they will eliminate that old girlfriend of our Professor, Martha Reed, in Lansing. And that should take care of everything."

"Good, and the three of us will have a celebration in honor of the Fuhrer and Tojo after our mission is completed," the Governor gloated.

Hilda opened the door and yelled, "Wilhelm, come in. Take the professor and make sure that we don't see him anymore. Make sure his body isn't found."

Wilhelm lunged forward and grabbed Roy. As all eyes were on the struggle, Governor Hansler reached in his desk drawer and pulled out a .38 pistol with a silencer. He aimed toward Roy and Wilhelm, who was holding him from behind. Wilhelm let go of Roy and stepped aside, to let the Governor have a clear shot at him.

The Governor, instead, deliberately aimed at Wilhelm and shot him in the midsection. Hilda shouted, "he's gone crazy, stop him, stop him!" She picked up a marble bookend and heaved it at her brother. Governor Hansler shot Hilda in the head; she fell over dead. Takeda turned and ran for the door, but Hansler fired twice killing him instantly. The shot did not disable Wilhelm and he managed to grab the Governor around the neck and wrestled for the gun. They staggered to the porch railing where Governor Hansler squeezed the trigger once more as Wilhelm jerked his arm, breaking the Governor's neck. The weight of the two men broke through the railing and they tumbled to the hillside below.

Clayton ran toward the porch steps as soon as he heard the first shot. But, it all happened so fast that when he reached the living room, Roy was standing there in a daze. Clayton could see two dead bodies on the floor, and he had seen the two men flying over the railing as he dashed up the stairway at the end of the porch.

"I can't believe it, he did it to save me... he tried to save me...the Governor, it was his plan, it worked, except...he's gone," Roy was mumbling.

Clayton snapped Roy out of his trance and they climbed down the hillside under the porch. Governor

Hansler's last shot had gone right through Wilhelm's heart. Roy climbed along the hillside to the Governor's body. He found his wallet and inside was Eda's list. Roy put the wallet back, but took the list with him. He and Clayton continued down to the dock, jumped into the Nicolet, and returned to Roy's cottage. It was almost midnight.

Roy was exhausted mentally and physically. He and Clayton fell asleep after discussing the unbelievable night. When Roy woke up early on Wednesday morning it was like a dream, or more like a nightmare.

The bodies had been discovered early Wednesday morning by the landscaper. The Secret Service had scheduled their protection of the new candidate for the Vice-Presidency to begin the following week. After all, he had just been selected. They and the State Police had rushed to the Island to investigate the multiple killings.

After a preliminary investigation, the news story on the television and in the newspapers described the scene.

The Detroit News-Free Press reported:

"On Tuesday evening, Governor Raymond Hansler, selected by President Barnes and nominated by the Republican Party at last week's convention as candidate for the Vice-Presidency, was killed on Mackinac Island. His death was apparently due to a fall from the front porch of the Governor's Summer Residence.

The bodies of Mr. Ito Takeda, Director of the Japanese Global Trade Organization, and those of two employees of the Mansion were also found. Mr. Takeda and Hilda Schwartz, housekeeper, were shot to death. The body of Mr. Wilhelm Schmidt, caretaker, was found next to that of the Governor. He too died of gunshot wounds. Police are baffled. The local police, arriving at the scene on their bicycles, automatically waived jurisdiction to the State Police. The Governor's Summer Residence is itself, part of a state park. The police will only say that the case is under investigation."

Then Roy shouted, "Clayton, it's Wednesday, I have to get to Honolulu, now!" Clayton hadn't known about Takeda's plans until Roy quickly explained. "Amos and Andy will be in Honolulu on Wednesday or Thursday to kill Luana, Takeda said, and then they will go to Lansing to kill Martha, and then here to take care of you."

Roy dressed and packed for the trip while he was planning what to do. "I can drive to Lansing faster than getting the next plane out of Pellston. You call Martha and tell her I am coming. I will definitely call you and Martha by Thursday, it'll be six hours later here, so it will be late Thursday. If we don't stop them, heaven forbid for Luana's sake, you must go to Martha and get some protection for both of you."

Roy called Robert at the China Garden, "Hello Robert, I'll explain as soon as I get there, but Luana is in immediate danger. Can you protect her until I get there? I'll be on the United flight one from Chicago arriving at seven o'clock." Robert assured Roy that he would take care of everything.

•

Roy met Martha at 1:45 p.m. at the Lansing airport. She said, "the plane leaves at 2:45 so we have some time before you board. Let's grab a snack. Martha had a bagel with cream cheese with her coffee; Roy had no appetite, just his usual thirst for coffee. Roy briefed her on the danger and gave her a detailed description of the massacre on Mackinac Island.

"Martha, will you leak this version to the press, anonymously, if possible. And let Pam tell the news about Eda's meeting with her and the others. That would verify that Takeda was a 'yakuza' agent. Whichever way you decide, let the police and the public know that Takeda, joined forces with Hilda and Wilhelm, who were active followers of the Nazi movement, and that Governor Hansler discovered it somehow. They threatened, and must have tried, to kill him. He managed to grab the gun from one of them, and was able to shoot Hilda and Takeda. He wounded Wilhelm, who was able to lift him up to throw him over the railing, but it broke and they both fell to their death. The Governor was a hero; he risked, and ended up giving his life, instead of acquiescing to the demands of an international crime syndicate."

Martha became somber, "there is something I have to tell you; I hope you won't be mad at me?" She didn't wait for an answer. "I have a good friend in the FAA. I asked him to check the remains of the flight Eleanor was on for anything unclaimed or any clue at all. He found this set of keys among the items still remaining. The tag is burned, but you can see what looks like an E right here, see?"

Roy's heart beat rapidly, he recognized Eleanor's keys. One of the charred keys had a partially visible, yellow top. All of the cottage door keys had yellow tops to match the cottage. Roy had it done so that when his boys came to the cottage they could easily identify, and wouldn't forget to bring, their own key. Tears came to Roy's eyes. Eleanor was dead. She was gone; only to Heaven and to her precious Jesus, of course, but gone to Roy, here and now. Eleanor was such a strong Christian that Roy didn't worry about her soul, but he was grieving inside. Since he hadn't accepted her death before, this was the time of her death for him.

"I'm sorry, Martha, I never accepted it before now, without some proof." He had a hard time talking.

"I know, I understand," Martha was becoming weepy in sympathy for Roy.

They both regained their composure and Martha tried to say something humorous. "I just did it so I could have you for myself, ha!, ha!" She realized that her statement was not funny, because there was some truth in it. She knew that Roy couldn't break loose from Eleanor until he had that proof of her death. But, she also knew that it was Luana, not she, who would benefit from her detective work.

"Martha, you are a wonderful friend. Oh, before I leave, you and Clayton must be careful. Don't take any chances. I called Robert to help, so I'll have protection the moment I arrive in Honolulu. As soon as we trace Amos and Andy, I'll call you and Clayton."

Martha said, "OK, thanks, and Roy, I must tell you this. I think Luana is in love with you."

Roy shied away from the reality of this truism, "but she's like a kid to me."

Martha snapped, "Roy, she's 38 years old. That's not a kid. But, I don't want to tell you what your own feelings are. To tell the truth, I would rather have you fall in love with me, no... really... I would. I've grown more than fond of you. But, look at me, 48 years old, and well... that's old for a woman."

"Martha, you're gorgeous, you look like a twenty year old," Roy exaggerated. "But, you're right, I don't even know my own feelings yet. But, I do know one thing; I love you like a sister. I can't change that; it's an ironclad feeling I've always had about you since childhood. Our type of spiritual friendship is better than any other, even an intimate, physical one."

Martha would have said if she had swallowed a spoonful of truth syrup, "I won't buy that." But she just smiled and said, "You're right Roy. I guess that's really the way I feel about you too; but sometimes I mistake it for a different kind of love."

It was time to board. Martha and Roy gave each other a bear hug. Martha gave him a kiss on the cheek, and Roy turned to board the flight for Chicago and Honolulu. Martha took out her handerchief when Roy disappeared from sight.

•

Almost an hour before reaching Honolulu, Roy finally dozed off. Then he opened his eyes, and was standing on the enclosed porch of the cottage, looking out at the water. Roy heard a noise at the other end of the cottage and saw the door swing open. Eleanor wiped her shoes on the mat, walked in the main room and laid some books on the Rittenhouse table.

"Oh my God, Eleanor... I thought you were... what happened; where have you been?

"Roy, you know I was at the church women's retreat for the last three days. I told you all about it."

Roy put his arms around her and held her tight; he could feel her arms around him, so permanent, like she would never let go. After a full minute, she stepped back and held his hands, "I just came back to let you know that everything is alright, I'm fine."

She kissed Roy gently on the lips and walked back to the door. "I have to hurry; I'm leaving on another retreat; this one will be longer. You know that I will always love you, Roy; but don't wait for me." Eleanor picked up the books, closed the door behind her and walked away.

Roy was startled by a voice, "this is Captain Miller speaking. We are beginning the landing approach to the Honolulu International Airport. Those on the right side of the plane will be able to see the crater of Diamondhead, the hotels and beaches at Waikiki, and downtown Honolulu. I'm turning on the fasten your seat belts signal; we should be on the ground in ten minutes. I hope you've enjoyed you travel with United."

Oh, that beautiful feeling of being in paradise whenever the airplane circled for a landing at Honolulu International Airport. The lush green hills of Manoa Valley, the blue-green waters of Pearl Harbor, and the universally recognized shape of Diamondhead in the distance; it couldn't be on this earth. It was just turning dusk at 7:00 P.M. Honolulu time.

Roy's transcendental experience was much too real. He knew that it really happened, but only to him and Eleanor. It was Eleanor's way of telling him it was alright. He needed help in letting go, and she was the only one who could do it for him.

25

THE Fujima reached the Honolulu Harbor next to the Aloha Tower at 6:00 p.m. Captain Taro Ozeki had a cargo of repair parts for the Japanese-made rental automobiles. They would remain in the harbor for three days. The crew had to go through customs in order to enjoy the fun they would have in Chinatown. Waikiki was for the tourists; Chinatown had more attractions for the experienced seamen. Roy had asked Robert to meet him at the baggage area. Robert had his own car, a 1988 Buick LeSabre, at the curb. Roy briefed him as they drove to

Wo Fat's, where they went directly to the Information Network Center.

George Tong said, "Nice to see you again Professor Nelson."

Roy smiled and then turned serious, "I'm glad to see you, too, more than you realize. I'm afraid I'm in a hurry. Amos and Andy are going to kill Luana, and we have to stop them. Do you know where they are?"

It was Robert who explained, "when they, Amos and Andy, get on the Fujima, we have no way of tracking them. We had an informer on the ship two months ago, but he just disappeared. The Fujima docked here about an hour ago. No one has come through customs, yet. You are just in time to go... if you want to, that is, to the customs office and follow Amos and Andy if they attempt to go into Honolulu. And we know that they will, if they are going to try to kill Miss Kameha."

George interrupted, "look at this, our computer has just identified two 'yakuza' agents, not by name; they got off the 7:30 flight from Tokyo."

Roy looked panic stricken.

"Don't worry, Professor," Robert quickly interjected. "Anyone who fits the 'yakuza' format is automatically followed. George, who is on duty tonight?"

"Kekua and Haunani are there. Wait a minute and I will contact them."

"Women? Roy questioned.

Robert cautioned, "professor, you wouldn't want to meet these two women in a dark alley if they were after you. They are the best we have."

Robert spoke to Roy in a serious tone, "this is what I want you to do. Go to the Royal Princess from here. Let's see, if you leave here in about fifteen minutes, you will be at the Pink Orchid Room at 9 o'clock. Miss Kameha is dancing there tonight as you know, and we have someone watching her right now. Sit at a table near the back and get her attention so she will sit with you during her intermissions. I'm sure you won't want to alarm her, but let her know what is going on."

"You two might have to move fast if we have any kind of a confrontation. Our job, as you already know, is not to use force. But in this case, we must thwart their deliberate attempt to kill one of our citizens. The police are just not organized to stop an international crime organization like the 'yakuza'."

Robert gave Roy his Buick to use and he drove to the Royal Hawaiian Shopping Center parking garage, which was the closest parking area to the Royal Princess, and parked on the third level. He took the elevator down to the street level and walked down Lewers Street to the Royal Princess.

The Pink Orchid Room had the most relaxing, informal, open setting you could imagine. The tables were generously spaced around a patio, so that the diners could arrange their chairs to watch the entertainment. Luana and the three musicians performed on a small platform beside a sprawling Monkey Pod tree. Behind the tree and the entertainers was the Pacific Ocean in all its splendor, and off to the left was the breathtaking silhouette of Diamondhead.

Roy sat at a table in the back. Luana was dancing and didn't see him. He ordered a cup of coffee and waited until Luana took a break. She always walked along the side of the patio and stopped to talk to friends, or tourists just anxious to talk to a beautiful Hawaiian girl. She stopped for a few minutes to talk and then resumed walking toward the back of the restaurant, where she had a dressing room for changing and resting between shows. She saw Roy standing next to his table, waiting for her to notice him. By this time she had resigned herself to their friendship status and was about to receive Roy's fatherly hug and to give him the traditional Hawaiian kiss on the cheek, maybe even both cheeks.

"Luana, I love you." He put his hands gently on each side of her head and slowly drew her lips to his in a soft, loving kiss, like that in the words of country western singer, K.T. Oslin, "don't kiss me like we're married, kiss me like we're lovers".

Her body, rigid in waiting for the expected hug around the shoulders, released all its inhibitions. Her voluptuous curves curled into Roy, this time expected, in fact, anticipated, filling all the empty spaces between them. Her body was soft and warm. Roy had forgotten how soft the body of a woman felt. Her deep brown eyes and moist lips sent enticing signals up and down his body. They embraced like a couple of teenage lovers.

Roy had deliberately picked a quiet spot in the back of the room so he wouldn't embarrass anyone with his show of emotion. Roy and Eleanor hated exhibitionists, and they had been horrified with the new style of kissing on the TV, where the actors seemed to eat each other's face, while the woman ripped the man's shirt off his back.

Roy's prudish dignity retired temporarily when Luana's exotic lips introduced him to an elevated dimension of sensuality.

"I love you too, Roy, but I thought you couldn't... I thought you weren't ready, because of..." Luana stumbled.

"It's alright, Luana, I'm free, now that I know that Eleanor is dead. I just couldn't before... it was like cheating...I don't know why, but that's me. I'm just old-fashioned I guess."

"I love you that way, don't ever change, Roy," Luana

said. "Oh, I have to change... my costume, that is," she giggled. "See you after the next break. Oh, you've made me so happy!"

Luana had just danced a fast Tahitian hula wearing a grass skirt, with her long black hair flowing. In the next, slow hula, she would wear a formal, black and white flowered Hawaiian mumu with a white flower in her hair, which would be put up in a tight bun. She was in her dressing room for longer than usual and the three musicians were noticeably irritated. They began to play without Luana. Robert tapped Roy on the shoulder.

"I'm sorry, Professor, they grabbed her in her dressing room and used her as a shield before we could shoot. They walked right out front and drove off. We have them followed and I am in constant contact. Where is the car?"

"Let's go," Roy responded. It's in the Royal Hawaiian lot down Lewers."

They ran all the way to the car on the third level, descended to the street level, and drove through the crowded streets of Waikiki. Robert was on his cellular phone.

"They're heading down King Street toward downtown Honolulu."

A few minutes later Robert said, "they turned on the Pali."

Roy knew! He knew what they planned. They already knew how to get rid of a body; over the Pali Lookout, where King Kamehameha chased his enemies over the cliff, and where they pushed Roy almost to his death. Roy shuddered with the horror of what might happen to his Luana. He just barely recovered from grieving for Eleanor, and now Luana.

"Robert, I think they are heading for the Pali Lookout. Can you get anyone there before them?" Roy pleaded.

Robert called the police. "There is a squad car near the entrance," he found out.

Roy said, "don't stop them at the entrance. Tell the police to go into the park and block the way from the parking lot to the cliff. That will give us enough time to get there and stop them."

Robert relayed the message.

Ten minutes later Mitsuo Fuchida and Saburo Shindo, the infamous Amos and Andy, were driving a white Town Car along the Pali Highway. In the back seat, Luana was tied and gagged. Shindo had a 'hachimaki', a white scarf, tied around his head. In an ancient tradition, the wives and sweethearts of the Japanese warriors gave them a 'hachimaki' when they went off to war. During the raid on Pearl Harbor, the Japanese pilots, along with their famous leaders, Fuchida and Shindo, wore their 'hachimaki's.

"Look," Amos said, "that police car turned in at the Lookout. Don't turn, keep going." Andy kept driving over the Koolau Mountains into the Pali tunnel and over to the Windward side.

Kekua Kalakaua and Haunani Nakea were Hawaiians, both graduates of the law enforcement program at Hawaii Pacific University. After leaving the Honolulu Harbor they were closer to the Pali than any other of Robert's associates. They were close behind the Town Car and saw them drive past the Lookout Drive. Haunani called Robert and Roy, who were only a mile behind.

"They just turned on the road toward Kailua."

Amos and Andy had turned onto a new section of the divided highway that led directly into the Kaneohe Marine Corps Air Station. They thought it was the highway that led to the Likelike Highway, which would take them back toward Honolulu and the Fujima. It was dark; the two drove right over a hill and there it was, the entrance to the Marine base with Guards stationed for in and out traffic. It was too late to turn around. Andy stepped on the accelerator and sped past the gate, the astonished guard gaping in disbelief at the speeding auto.

Close behind, Kekua and Haunani called the Military Police at the base and identified themselves. They received clearance for theirs and for Robert's car. An MP jeep joined the chase right behind Robert's car.

Andy followed the road around the outside of Mokapu Point that looked to him like the way out of the base. Roy knew where it went because he had been there before. It was a dead end. He had taught at the Kaneohe Marine Base twice before. They approached the base of the Ulupau Crater, the site of the small arms firing range, surrounded by a wire fence. Andy sped up and crashed through the gate. He was heading for the road to the outside wall of the crater. The road led to a flat landing about half way up the crater wall. There the road would end and they would be at the home of the Red-footed Booby Colony.

Robert called to Kekua and Haunani who had just reached the gate, "shoot over their heads just before the car stops."

When Haunani saw the brake lights come on she started shooting in the air above the Town Car. Robert was right, the shooting kept them so occupied that they forgot about Luana. Robert was afraid that if they had to abandon her they would kill her first. Amos and Andy were too busy to think about Luana as they scampered up the hillside.

Robert and Roy pulled up behind Kekua and Haunani's car. Roy jumped out and ran to the Town

Car, "Luana, Luana, are you alright?"

Luana mumbled something. Roy took off the 'hachimaki', which Amos had used to gag her and Luana gasped, "I'm OK."

He untied her and hugged her tight. "I was so worried, oh my God, if I had lost you after... after I just found you!"

Roy saw Kekua running toward the hill. "Stop her, Robert wait for me."

He turned to Luana, "I want you to go back to the main gate with one of the MP's, don't argue, and don't worry, I know what's up there and they don't."

Roy asked an MP to drive Luana to the main gate and wait for them. Neither Marine had been on top of Ulupau Crater, because it was normally off limits. Roy was the only person in the group who had been at the top. He remembered that there were no fences or signs at the edge of the cliffs or at the turret of the Arizona.

He spoke to Robert, the MP and the two women, "it's dangerous up there; you could easily fall over a cliff in the dark. Always stay within ten feet of me, don't wander away. Do you have a flashlight?"

The Marine had two heavy-duty lamps. Roy took one and led the way up the hill. The Boobies were resting in their perches all around them as they climbed the steep side of the crater. Haunani almost stepped on a Mongoose that scampered noisily into the brush. It was patiently waiting for a helpless Baby Booby to fall out of its nest.

They reached the top with its breathtaking view. On one side, the Koolau Mountains, like shadowy, deep green stalagmites, and on the other, the white tops of the ocean waves, glistening in the moonlight, was a sight that tourists would love to see, but the Boobies and the Marines had their reservations in first.

Roy slowly moved through the thick, tree-like bushes used as perches by the Boobies toward the edge of the cliff. He cautioned the group to stay behind him. Roy knew there were no fences at the edge of the cliff so he continually flashed the light ahead of them. When Roy spotted the edge he stopped the group and crawled on all fours. It was several hundred feet to the rocks below. Roy saw something large on the beach when the water receded from the huge waves splashing on the rocks below.

"Robert, could that be a body down there?"

Robert crawled to the edge and looked down. "It's too far to tell; it could be, or it could be a large fish. I can't tell for sure."

"Well we can't do anything about it from up here. Let's move toward the other end. Stay close and stay behind me. Have you heard any noise anywhere?"

None of them had seen or heard anything in the brush. They proceeded slowly when Roy saw a dark figure stand up in the brush about fifty yards ahead. The man shot at them once, turned away and ran. Roy could hear him yell what sounded like, "ayiii", and then silence. Roy lead the group, cautiously, to the edge of the Arizona's turret and Roy flashed his light down the three story cement caisson. At the bottom were jagged pieces of metal, blown apart by the explosions in 1941.

"There he is, it's Amos, Fuchida, that is." Roy could see his face.

Mitsuo Fuchida lay dead inside the big-gun turret, salvaged from the battleship, Arizona, which in 1941 was mercilessly bombed by the first wave of Japanese planes, led by none other than his namesake uncle, Mitsuo Fuchida. His uncle didn't die in the raid. He lived for almost two decades longer.

A few minutes later, two jeeps brought more Marines

to help in the search. Roy, Robert, Kekua and Haunani went down to the cave level while the Marines kept up the search for another forty-five minutes. The Marine party searched inside the cave and over the sides of the crater wall. Another Marine party looked at the bottom of the cliff where Roy thought he saw something, but they found no sign of another body. They concluded that if it was Shindo's body, it could have washed out to sea.

Roy thanked Kekua and Haunani and the Marines. There was nothing more they could do. They returned to the gate to get Luana. Robert, Roy and Luana drove back over the Pali to Honolulu.

Roy tried to alleviate Luana's concern, "Don't worry about Shindo, Luana; even if that wasn't his body, Hilda and Takeda are dead now, so his mission will be cancelled. What do you think, Robert?"

"I agree, Roy, and we continually monitor the 'yakuza' so if he is alive, he will show up in our system, sooner or later."

"I'll talk to you tomorrow, Robert. I can't thank you enough for what you've done."

"Forget it, Professor, all in a day's work," Robert kidded.

"Isn't it time you called me Roy."

Robert said, "OK Roy, I will." Robert drove them to Luana's apartment on Ala Moana Boulevard and dropped them off.

26

A T last, Roy and Luana were alone. But Luana couldn't leave him alone. She hugged him and kissed him, like a little girl raiding the cookie jar with impunity. Roy, a captive of propriety, loved it. He was experiencing and thoroughly enjoying the uninhibited affection of Luana's oriental culture, a far cry from the stoic Scandinavian and English culture in which he was raised.

"Let's get married," Roy stated or asked. "I'm... having a hard time staying away from you. I mean... I want to love you completely. But, you know me, I want it to be right. I still believe that true love can wait for the formality of God's marriage vows."

"You sound like a preacher," Luana chided him. "I'm going to drag you to the bedroom right now," and she started to pull her torn, dirty mumu up over her head, partially revealing the more provocative lingerie she wears only with her dressy costumes.

"Wait," Roy meekly objected.

"Oh, I'm just kidding. Do you expect me keep this horrible thing on? I'm going to take a shower, and if I feel like taking my clothes off in my own apartment you'll just have to close your eyes or go in another room. After all, we're going to be married soon. You shouldn't be afraid of me. I have a normal body just like any other woman."

Roy closed his eyes just in time as the former Miss Honolulu pulled the black and white mumu all the way off and stood in front of him in her panties and bra. She had her high heels on, which augmented the already impeccable quality of her figure. But Roy missed it all; he didn't even peek.

"I'm going to make some coffee, if I can find the kitchen with my eyes closed. Do you want some, too?"

"OK, after my shower."

Roy opened his eyes when he found the kitchen and began making the coffee. He inadvertently walked to the kitchen door to say something when he saw her standing there in her lingerie and heels. He quickly closed his eyes, but the image remained for some time.

After her shower Luana stopped teasing Roy. She wore a conservative nightgown and covered that with a robe. They were both pretty exhausted. Coffee late at night didn't seem to bother either one of them. But this night, sleeping in the guest room, Roy had a restless night. It wasn't the coffee, it was the image of Luana. He wanted the wedding to be soon.

The next morning Luana made the coffee and the two sat and looked at each other. Luana said, "before I say yes, I have a confession to make."

She smiled, "you have the right to withdraw your proposal. I have never been married, but...", she hesitated.

"Go on, I'm a big boy; you're not going to shock me... Roy grinned, " I hope!"

"Well, I... had a wild period just after I became Miss Honolulu, about two years. Roy, please understand that I was... young and naive... and you can't imagine the way some men take advantage of beauty queens. Flowers, jewelry... and I didn't realize it had a price. Roy... I had an affair, that is... you know what I mean, I lived with a man, a wealthy man, for almost a year."

"And of course if you lived with him, that means you slept with him. Was there only one man?"

"Well... no. Wait, it isn't as bad as it sounds. I liked the gifts and being in with the wealthy crowd. But, I didn't love him at all. I dropped him, or he became bored with me, I think it was mutual. Later, I did... kind of... fall in love with another man. That affair lasted about six months, before I found out what a creep he was. Remember, I was only in my early twenties. I never got the chance to grow up, Roy, if I were... if I were fat and ugly this wouldn't have happened."

"Luana! Don't rationalize; you know you're responsible for your own actions. But, you haven't told me anything that would change my opinion of you. You made mistakes and so have I, and as far as I'm concerned you have nothing to be ashamed of. Besides, I love you, and that takes precedence over everything else. Now Luana will you say yes to my proposal?"

"Oh yes!... Roy... you... are... the... sweetest," smothering him with intermittent kisses.

Later that day Roy called Clayton and Martha and told them about the end of the 'yakuza' threat. He asked them to stand up at their wedding. They both agreed and would be on a plane as soon as arrangements could be made for their absence.

Back in Lansing, State Senator Pam Lehto had a news conference. The Lansing State News and the other state papers and the TV stations carried this story:

Mystery At Mackinac Solved

The mystery at Mackinac Island, where four people, including Governor Raymond Hansler, were killed is solved. State Senator Pam Lehto revealed the details of a secret meeting at the State Capitol Building on July 15 with Governor Hansler, the Japanese Minister of Trade, Tomizo Eda, State Senators Trump and Lehto and five European trade ministers. Senator Lehto said that Mr. Eda warned them that Mr. Ito Takeda, Director of the Japanese Global Trade Organization, was a member and representative of the Japanese 'yakuza', which is the equivalent of the mafia. Mr. Eda said that he would give Governor Hansler a list of the 'yakuza'-owned Japanese companies that wanted to build plants in the U.S. The next day Mr. Eda was murdered by a 'yakuza' professional killer, and the list disappeared.

On July 20, at the Governor's Mansion on Mackinac Island, Takeda and two members of the Nazi Movement in America, a Mrs. Hilda Schwartz, posing as housekeeper, and a Mr. Wilhelm Schmidt, also known as William Smith, posing as groundskeeper, threatened the Governor if he didn't obey their demands. When Governor Hansler refused, they attempted to shoot him.

The Governor managed to grab the gun from the

assailants and to shoot and kill Mrs. Schwartz and Takeda. Schmidt, who was wounded, wrestled with the Governor until they both plunged over the front porch railing. The Governor managed to fatally shoot Schmidt, but he too was killed in the struggle or by the fall from the porch.

Governor Hansler knew that the 'yakuza'-owned companies were planning to undermine the legitimate U.S. automobile parts industry. The Nazi followers knew that their cause would be strengthened if the 'yakuza' gained control. Many 'yakuza' crime family members want to bring back the memories of 'Tojo' and Japanese superiority, just as the Nazi followers want to revive memories of Hitler and the 'super race'. The secret list was mailed to Senator Lehto, anonymously. She has turned it over to the FBI.

This week the State flag will be flown at half mast to honor the memory of Governor Raymond Hansler, who sacrificed his life to preserve the freedoms that this great country, The United States of America, stands for.

On Saturday, August 15 the wedding was about to take place on the beach at Luana's parent's house in Waimanalo. Luana was dressed in a plain, but elegant white mumu.

"Clayton, have you ever been a best man before? Martha appeared to be provoking him into conversation.

"No, but I'll bet you've been a 'whatcha call it," a first lady, or whatever, a dozen times or so."

"It's a maid of honor, you dope. No, I've only done it two or three times."

"Well, make sure I do everything right. I'm not very good at this sort of thing, and with your experience you should know what to do."

"Ok, you're my protege from now on, Clayton." Martha

thought that might make him feel more assured.

Tamar and Walter were pleased with their daughter's choice. Walter was an unobtrusive man who liked anyone who was not aggressive, so he had no trouble liking good-natured Roy.

It was a simple wedding, with Clayton, Martha and Luana's favorite relatives on beautiful Waimanalo Beach. Luana's father and uncles roasted a pig for an authentic Hawaiian luau and the dancing and singing went on all evening. Roy and Luana could at last relax in the peaceful setting around them. They sat on the beach with Clayton and Martha who were getting to like each other, and reminisced about the events of the last three months. There was a lot to laugh about, and a lot to be sad about. They were the only people on Earth who knew the truth about Hitler's children, and they could tell no one. The four of them vowed that it had to remain a secret forever to protect the honor of the man who saved Roy's life.

"But," Martha said, "I wish we knew the truth. Most historians agree that Hitler didn't have any children and some say there is evidence that he couldn't have. But several doctors said that about my one of my cousins, and bingo, not long after he and his wife adopted a child, they had one of their own. So how can we trust second and third hand information from back in 1939 and 40. The very fact that Eva Braun was banned from public appearances with Hitler during the time the children would have been babies and toddlers indicates more than just coincidence."

"Not only that," added Clayton, "the secret that Toivo Makinen kept was never revealed to anyone, so how could the historians know the truth. The Russians confiscated almost all the Hitler records before the Allies even got there."

"I think we've beaten that subject to death," Roy said. "Let's talk about the food."

They all laughed and talked about lighter subjects. At 11 o'clock, the guests were still going strong, but Roy yawned conspicuously among the guests. Roy said, "we've really had a busy day, Tamar, I think Luana and I had better get some sleep."

Roy didn't fool Luana, or anyone else for that matter. Roy and Luana waved goodby to everyone and drove off to her apartment for the night. Roy asked, "Luana, did you think I was too old-fashioned, you know, about last night? I was kind of prudish and you actually made me blush. You're really too good for me, you know."

"Roy, I love you because of the way you are. And about the other night, it wasn't nice of me to tease you the way I did, but you don't think I would have let you get any closer, do you?"

"I'll never know, will I? By the way, you won't be able to dance at the Royal Princess if you're in Michigan with me. Is that going to be hard for you?"

"Don't worry, I'll adjust, as long as I'm with you."

"This was going to be a surprise, but I can't keep it a secret any longer." Roy irritatingly dangled the statement in front of her and stopped.

Luana waited impatiently, "well?"

"The University of Hawaii has offered me a position as Visiting Professor of Management Accounting beginning this Fall semester; should I take it?"

"Oh Roy, that's wonderful, but don't do it for me. I'll be happy, whatever!"

"Well, it's only for one year, so after that its back to Michigan and my Whitefish sandwiches."

27

SABURO Shindo was running a few feet from his friend Mitsuo Fuchida. He heard Fuchida shoot at their pursuers and watched in horror when Fuchida disappeared over the edge of Penn Battery, the Arizona's turret. A hundred feet or so ahead he almost ran into the machine gun enclosure, which stuck up about four feet above the ground level. He climbed inside to hide and discovered the ladder. Shindo climbed down three flights into absolute darkness and felt around until he found a doorway. He pushed open the door and saw a trickle of light at the end of a long open area. Heading for the light Andy saw the huge plastic bubble at the entrance of the cave.

Shindo walked outside and disappeared into the brush. He climbed around the ocean side of the crater wall until he found an opening to the water. The fairly calm waters made it possible to swim across to the sandy shoreline at Kailua Beach Park. The Marines were still searching for him at the top of Ulupau Crater. Andy managed to steal a rusty 1978 Ford pickup and drove toward Honolulu. He stopped to get some money at a bank money machine in Kahala.

On Saturday, the day of the wedding, the Fujima left the Honolulu Harbor without Matsuo Fuchida and Saburo Shindo. Captain Taro Ozeki maintained his schedule without regard for his 'yazuka' hitchhikers. Amos and Andy were not the only "yakuzas' who travelled on the Fujima. Captain Ozeki knew that his two proteges would finish the job that Takeda had ordered. He wondered why he hadn't heard from Takeda, perhaps when he reached the St. Lawrence Seaway, which was the usual place for receiving his instructions.

•

The following Monday morning Roy woke up at 9:00 a.m. and made coffee. He took a cup into the bedroom and made enough noise to wake Luana. He handed her an envelope with a Robert's Overnighter travel voucher for three days on the Big Island, Hawaii.

"I thought we could be alone for a few days, and we could see the volcanoes. What do you think?"

"I'd love it; I haven't been there since the Volcano House was destroyed at Kilauea. Where are we staying?

"At the Kona Hilton; it's part of the package and I like the way almost every room faces the ocean. We can drive to the volcanoes and back in one day from Kona."

Luana and Roy took an Aloha Airlines flight that afternoon to Keahole Airport, picked up their rental car and drove the eight miles to Kailua-Kona. They checked in at the Kona Hilton at four-thirty. Roy had arranged for a deluxe room; the two newlyweds had a leisurely dinner at the hotel and spent the rest of the evening thoroughly enjoying each other. On Tuesday morning, after breakfast at the Kona Ranch House in town, they set out for Volcanoes National Park.

Back in Honolulu, Robert and George were at Wo Fat's. Robert had just received a call at the restaurant from George, "Robert, I'm at Wo Fat's, you'd better come here right away."

Robert knew that meant don't ask questions, just come, "alright, I'll be there in twenty minutes."

George said, "look at this, Andy just turned up at the Bank of Honolulu in the Kahala Shopping Center. Robert and George had one procedural secret that they kept to themselves, mainly for security reasons. Their system used air, train, rental car and other modes of travel as the basis of their monitoring system, which allowed 'Yakuza' members to easily escape the computers for short periods of time.

But George had devised a plan to trace the use of bank money cards. He and Robert had high level contacts in cooperating countries to obtain bank numbers of the 'yakuza' and other mafia members. Their contact in Japan was Tomizo Eda. Robert and George with the help of friends in Japan, had provided the 'list' which Eda took to Lansing, in return for bank cooperation.

International criminals, like Amos and Andy, never used charge accounts, which could easily be traced.

They used bank money cards for their cash. George's computers were able to trace a 'yakuza' member whenever he used his card. Andy had used his card in the bank machine in Kahala, and Bingo! George's computers nailed him to the spot and the time.

"Well, now we know that he's alive and is on Oahu, or was yesterday," Robert concluded from George's computer which showed the time of the cash withdrawal.

"You'd better tell Roy right away," George said.

"He and Luana are on the Big Island, on their honeymoon. I'll call Tamar; she'll know where to leave a message."

"Tamar, this is Robert. Would you leave a message with Roy to call me at the restaurant; it's important."

"Oh sure, Robert; you're the second one who called today about the newlyweds."

"Who else asked, Tamar?"

"A friend of Roy's...he said he was a friend, anyway, he called and asked where he could send them some flowers. I said they were staying at the Kona Hilton and that they were going to see the volcanoes, that's all. He said thanks and hung up. Did I do something wrong?"

"No, Tamar, don't worry. I'll take care of everything," Robert assured her. Robert was on the next Aloha Airlines flight to the Keahole Airport on the Big Island, the island of volcanoes and Madame Pele.

Roy and Luana reached Kealakekua Bay, the site of Captain Cook's massacre by the natives in 1779. As they drove toward Naalehu, the Southernmost town in the United States, the coastline became blacker with the folds of hardened lava flows. They drove up Crater Road, like driving on the moon, until they reached the Visitor's Center in the National Park. They stopped for information and decided to drive around Crater Rim Road which circled Kilauea Caldera.

Luana and Roy drove to the parking lot in front of Halemaumau Crater, 3,000 feet in diameter and 1,700 feet deep. Madame Pele is believed to reside in Halemaumau. They walked to Lookout Point at the edge of the crater. There were no other people there except a woman in a tattered blue mumu wearing a wide-brimmed hat. She was kneeling at the edge and was placing a small bunch of orchids, a half empty bottle of coke, and two bananas on the ground.

"She is appeasing Pele," Luana explained to Roy. "Some of the superstitious Hawaiians still fear Pele and make these sacrifices so she won't harm them and their families. Even Mother still believes in the powers of Madame Pele. You could never convince her that Pele is just a myth."

As if to justify her mother's rationality, Luana added, "When Kilauea and Mauna Loa both erupted together in 1984, for the first time in over a hundred years, there were several sightings of Pele. During the eruptions, she was reportedly seen on three separate occasions. A man and wife reported that they encountered a woman in a green mumu with flowers over both ears on a desolate stretch of road near the eruptions. She said she was Pele and asked for a drink. They gave her some juice and she disappeared in front of them. The papers even printed several pictures of Pele's face in the clouds over the eruption vent."

Roy remembered his first trip with Eleanor to the Big Island. They toured the volcanoes and Roy had picked up some samples of volcanic rock to take home to show the boys. By the time they reached the Keahole Airport Roy had heard so many stories of bad luck and plane crashes due to taking Pele's rocks, he tossed all the rocks on the ground before taking off. Eleanor just smiled at him and didn't say a word.

Luana and Roy didn't notice that there was a white scarf wrapped around the battered old blue ribbon on the woman's hat. She stood up and walked past Luana and Roy as they approached the edge of the crater. They stood there looking at the awesome hole in the earth, when all of a sudden the sun just seemed to disappear. Roy glanced skyward to see the black and gray clouds swirling into a formation directly above. A woman's face appeared in the center of the cloud formation, and even Roy, instinctively assumed that it was the face of Madame Pele.

The face wasn't smiling, it was more like anger, no, more like a warning in her face. It looked as if her arm was outstretched, her finger pointing at him or through him, past him, behind him. He involuntarily turned his head around and caught a glimpse of movement from behind him.

The skirt of the blue dress was fluttering from the force of the wind as a muscular body hurtled toward them with arms outstretched. Roy desperately grabbed for Luana's shoulders and managed only to get a handful of her hair. He pulled her flat to the ground and fell on top of her.

The body of the woman in the blue mumu sailed over the edge of Madame Pele's favorite home, Halemaumau Crater in the Kilauea Caldera, to a violent death 1,700 feet below.

Luana and Roy lay on the ground for a full minute before getting up and brushing off the lava dust. After the horror of what might have happened wore off and the realization that the end of their long ordeal was finally over, Luana started laughing, and Roy couldn't help but join in.

"Why are we laughing?" Roy sputtered between laughs.

"Well, we've only been married three days, and here you are grabbing me by the hair, dragging me to the ground and jumping on top of me. What a way to start a marriage!"

This brought on a renewal of the laughing spell; then, suddenly they both stopped and Roy looked into Luana's enticing brown eyes.

"Let's go back to the hotel, don't you think?"

"How did you know what I was thinking?" Luana smiled.

When they returned to the Kona Hilton, Robert had just arrived.

"Roy, I have something important to tell you and Luana."

"Let me guess, Robert... let's see... your computers have located Andy, that is, Saburo Shindo, and you followed him here, to the Big Island, and you came to warn us, right."

"Well, yes, I guess that's it, almost, but how did you know?"

"Robert, if you tell your police friends to retrieve the body at the bottom of Halemaumau Crater, you should be able to take Andy off your computers for good."

Roy knew that he could never tell anyone, except maybe Tamar, how Madame Pele had taken her final revenge for the bombing of Pearl Harbor, and the destruction caused to her sacred land.

The next morning, after learning of the events at Halemaumau Crater, Tamar took her usual walk along Waimanalo Beach. She instinctively looked up when the clouds began swirling above Ulupau Crater at the Kaneohe Marine Air Corps Station. She sensed the presence of Madame Pele. But, for the first time, the clouds were not dark and ominous as they formed the face of Pele. And this time Tamar was not mystified by the Madame's rare smile. She knew that Pele was finally happy, she had avenged the bombing of her precious land.